A PLACE OF SKULLS
and other tales

David Ludford

Parallel Universe Publications

First Published in the UK in 2016
Copyright © 2016 David Ludford
Cover design © 2016

A Place of Skulls © 2016 originally published in *Schlock!* Vol 9 17th edition
Ain't No Grave Can hold My Body Down © 2015 originally published in *Schlock!* Vol 8 Issues 20 to 21
Almost Human © 2016 originally published in *Schlock!* Vol 10, Issue 5 3
Bonestaff © 2015 originally published in *Schlock!* Vol 8, Issue 15
Bridesmaids © 2015 originally published in *Schlock!* Vol. 9, Issue 2
Dummies © 2013 originally published in *Schlock!* Vol. 5, Issue 15
Heretics, Neophytes & Nemesis © 2015 originally published in *Schlock!* Vol. 8, Issue 28
Killing Clowns © 2015 originally published in *Schlock!* Vol. 9, Issue 2
The Bone Collector © 2016 originally published in *Schlock!* Vol. 10, Issue 3
Sleepwalker © 2015 originally published in *Schlock!* Vol 8, 18th edition
The Box © 2016 originally published in *Schlock!* Vol 9, 16 edition
The Burning Tree © 2016 originally published in *Schlock!* Vol 9, 9 edition

ISBN: 978-0-9935742-6-9
Parallel Universe Publications, 130 Union Road,
Oswaldtwistle, Lancashire, BB5 3DR, UK

CONTENTS

A PLACE OF SKULLS

"…every dream will reveal itself as a psychological structure, full of significance, and one which may be assigned to a specific place in the psychic activities of the waking state."

Freud: *The Interpretation of Dreams*

To Janic it was a recurring nightmare. He was standing in the middle of a vast field where no crops grew and no birds sang overhead, and the only sound was that of a soft, susurrating breeze. He was surrounded by skulls of varying ages and sizes: some were of adults, others of children that stretched away to the horizon on all sides. He was alone, and the loneliness cut through him making his whole body ache. He was certain that he was there as a punishment, although he was completely ignorant of what crime he may have committed. The nightmare always ended in the same way: overhead, in the branches of an ancient oak, a crow began to roar a tremendous, throaty croak that resounded like an everlasting condemnation and judgement. Then he woke up.

Almost midday: the morning had been long and slow, and Janic had been devoid of any distractions to take his mind off the nightmare, which he'd suffered again the previous night. A sense of impending doom – or at least of a dreadful revelation that would lead to some horrendous occurrence or experience – permeated his soul, to the core of his being. Standing in the bay window of his small flat, watching the slow procession of the world going by, he wondered with a feeling of mounting trepidation what fate had in store for him. His only question was: why now? During his thirty-six years on the planet he had experienced nothing like this before. He turned from the window and walked towards the small deal table next to his sofa and picked up the book he'd been desultorily reading for the last three weeks, but feeling that he'd not be able to give it his full concentration, put it down again with a heavy sigh. He wished that whatever was about to befall him would happen soon, if only to put him out of his abject misery. He was dreading the night to come.

This time the nightmare was different. As he stood surveying the grim scenario around him, he suddenly caught sight of a dark figure picking its way gingerly through the multitudinous skulls, making a haphazard progress towards him. As the figure came nearer, he could see that it was an elderly woman dressed in the black peasant garb of a bygone era. Her grey hair was long and unkempt and the expression on the heavily wrinkled, leathery skin of her face was one of deep sorrow. When she had drawn up to within twenty feet of him, she spoke in a voice that was cracked and weary, foregoing any sort of greeting or formalities.

"I expected you to come. You are not of this time, are you? Behold the sins of your illustrious ancestors." She gestured with both skinny, outstretched arms at their hellish surroundings, turning several times to encompass the whole scene. Then she became still, and was silent for several minutes before continuing, the bony index finger of one claw-like hand pointing directly at him:

"Are you proud of what Prince Berezovsky and his demon offspring the despot have done? Speak, stranger, so that I may understand the reasoning behind this carnage."

Janic tried to speak but his mouth was dry and his throat felt constricted. Once more, the crow launched into its horrendous, accusatory racket and he awoke: confused, bewildered and totally disorientated.

Dr Rachel Moretz was a psychotherapist who specialized in 'dream disorder', and had a small practice in a small back street off the main precinct in the town where Janic lived. She was the sister of Janic's ex-wife Helena; they had kept in regular touch as friends. There had been no bitterness or recriminations around the divorce, only a calm acceptance of the inevitable decline of the short-lived marriage, and Rachel had remained neutral, neither siding with her sister nor pouring blame upon Janic. She had

6

listened with professional interest as Janic had related his dream experiences to her over the phone and had readily agreed to see him, the appointment being made for the next day.

For the first twenty minutes of the session Rachel had insisted that Janic relate the dreams to her once more, which he had done, and Rachel saw the anxiety the recollections had caused him. Janic had then agreed to be hypnotized, and now lay prostrate on the couch, as Rachel calmly and quietly prompted her new patient to go back deep into his subconscious mind in an attempt to discover the root cause of the episodes. Janic, lying in silence for several minutes, suddenly began to relate an extraordinary narrative, his eyes tightly closed and his head intermittently moving slowly from side to side. Rachel clicked on her tape recorder.

"...chaos...Prince Berezovsky rules with an iron fist and is merciless...any who speak out against him are brutally slain. Our jails are full and bloody executions have become commonplace to make way for more prisoners...there's a never-ending supply...blood swills through the streets of the town, mixing with the filth and detritus of the gutters. The people are malnourished, impoverished...the prince and his court care nothing for them...men, women and children are dying in great numbers..."

During this short discourse Janic had become increasingly agitated, the movements of his head increased in speed and he had begun to thrash around wildly with his arms and legs. Rachel considered it a good time to bring proceedings to a halt. She stopped the tape, leaned close to Janic and snapped her fingers: Janic came to instantly, his eyes wide and staring. He was becalmed once more, and had a bewildered expression on his face. He rose slowly and swung his legs off the couch but remained sitting there. Rachel moved back behind her desk, tape recorder in hand. She looked very concerned.

"What have I been babbling on about?" Janic asked, seeing Rachel's look. Rachel was silent for some moments before answering:

"You have been telling me some extraordinary things, Janic. Bizarre, even. Listen to this."

She rewound the tape and hit 'play'.

Janic heard a voice, which at first didn't seem recognizable as his own. His expression of bewilderment increased as he listened intently to the words. When the tape had finished, he said, with a shocked expression on his face:

"What do you make of it, Rachel? What was it all about? That was crazy."

"Not at all crazy," Rachel replied. "I believe it is something that has long been buried deep in your subconscious mind. We'll need to have more sessions in order to learn more. But not today; I think you've been through enough for now. I must say that I'm intrigued by it, though."

"It sounded like something that happened in a past life. Something bad, something evil…and there was mention of a Prince Berezovsky; that's who the old woman referred to in my dream; more specifically the fact that this guy was my ancestor."

Rachel nodded her head slowly.

"Indeed. Janic, how much do you know of your family history, or where you're from?"

"Virtually nothing," he replied. "My grandparents on my father's side fled here as refugees from some obscure eastern European country to escape some kind of purge. They spoke very little of it, as if doing so caused them great pain. They died when I was still quite young. My father, too, was quite reluctant to talk about what little he had learned about his parents' former life. One thing I do remember, he told me that since he was a young boy he'd been afflicted by strange, recurring nightmares that began after my grandfather passed away. More than that he wouldn't say; but they had an incapacitating effect on him, like depression. I'm wondering…"

Rachel waited patiently for Janic to continue.

"…it sounds insane, Rachel, but is it possible that we can inherit dreams? Or, in this case, to be more exact, nightmares? This is a long shot but I'm wondering if my nightmares are the same, or similar, to the ones my father suffered. Could he have unwillingly – and unwittingly – passed them down to me? Are they destined to be passed down the generations until whatever sin or evil they are concerned with is atoned for?"

Rachel blew out her cheeks, stood up and walked slowly to the wide windows of her office, her back therefore towards Janic.

After a few minutes silence, she turned to face her patient, but still remained standing where she was.

"Interesting theory, Janic…very interesting. I've never come across it before and there is no precedent or similar case that I'm aware of. I'll search through my books and do an internet trawl. It's incredible to think it may be possible, or does actually happen. Perhaps by talking about it, bringing these repressed incidents to the forefront of your consciousness, will act as a kind of catharsis."

Janic smiled grimly.

"Or, in this case, a kind of exorcism. I hope you're right, Rachel, I really do. After the nightmares, I've been waking up exhausted, mentally and physically. I can't concentrate; they are seeping into every aspect of my life like some malignant evil. I just want them to stop, to 'appease the spirits' or whatever it is that I have to, need to do."

Janic left Rachel's office ten minutes later, having made a further appointment the day after next. His mind was racing as he walked the short distance home as he considered what the nightmares could mean, and how they would potentially continue to afflict his life. He felt like a condemned man heading for an execution; like someone on death row, and had the further feeling that things were coming to a head, that whatever was the significance of the nightmares and the impact they would have on his life would be made known very soon. Along the way he stopped at an off licence and bought a bottle of brandy, the mad thought having come to him that maybe the evil in his subconscious state could be expunged by the cleansing power of alcohol.

That evening Janic did his own internet trawl while sipping from a glass of the fiery, warming and calming spirit. He'd started by typing 'the history of east European countries' into his search engine but this had brought up so much information that he immediately felt overwhelmed and lost. He began again, this time typing 'Prince Berezovsky'. This too brought up lots of information but he felt that he'd narrowed and refined the search

9

down to more relevant specifics. He clicked randomly onto one of the links, the text of a geographical journal dated twenty years previously, and began to read. Despite the pleasurable effects of the alcohol, these were soon replaced by an icy chill that numbed his whole body and made him shiver.

The basic facts, which he summarized in his head having read just a few pages, were that Prince Berezovsky had been the 13th Century despotic ruler of a mountain kingdom called Krystania in what is now modern Bulgaria. He was believed to have been responsible for the slaughter of thousands of his own people in a brutal and bloody reign that lasted for two decades, until he was overthrown by a far superior armed force from a neighbouring kingdom, jealous of Krystania's mineral deposits which were its main source of wealth. Hundreds had also perished in Krystania's mines. Berezovsky was rumoured to be rather partial to the consumption of human flesh; other rumours had it that he was a vampire. He'd had one son and heir, Rapajic, who was desirous of following in his father's murderous footsteps and who avidly aided and abetted his father in his evil acts. Rapajic had managed to escape the chaos that followed the overthrow of his father, and had subsequently disappeared without trace. Nothing more was heard of the former royal family line for centuries until the 1920's, when a team of American historians from Boston University visited the region and tracked down Rapajic's bloodline, who were subsequently forced to flee the country or risk being murdered: the people of the region had passed down their desire for revenge through generations. They could not forget and certainly would never forgive.

Christ, Janic thought…that means my grandparents. They were somehow related to Berezovsky and Rapajic and fled for their lives. The 1920's was the decade my grandparents sought refuge in this country. Another thought struck him as he looked up from the screen and stared at the wall opposite; if Berezovsky lived and ruled in the 13th century, how many centuries had his family been suffering from the nightmares? The old woman in his dreams who had spoken to him had perhaps been a witch who had cursed his ancestors and subsequent generations until the crimes of Berezovsky and his son could be avenged. This whole thing was beginning to make some kind of bizarre sense. It *must* therefore be the case that dreams can be handed down from generation to generation… but where would it all end? If he were to have a son, would he too be similarly cursed if his father were somehow to escape retribution? He resolved to call Rachel the next morning, although perhaps she had come across the same information as he had and had drawn her own conclusions. He finished his drink, poured himself another large measure, and went up to bed, hoping the alcohol would have the desired effect but not really believing for one moment that it would.

He was wrong; Janic woke shortly after seven from a long, uninterrupted sleep. The nightmares hadn't come. He lay on his back, head lightly throbbing and with a distant low buzzing in his ears due to the brandy, but he was otherwise OK. He stared at the ceiling, daring to believe that somehow the curse on his family had been lifted. Perhaps the hypnosis had been the vital catalyst for this freedom from the nightmares, the lifting of the curse, and his subsequent exoneration from blame for the crimes of Berezovsky and Rapajic.

His thoughts were suddenly interrupted by the heavy pounding noise of padded feet rushing up his stairs: Valentino, his year-old Labrador, was coming to demand his early morning walk. Janic groaned, rolled over, and pulled the pillow over his head. But he knew there would be no escape; the dog wouldn't be put off. Never mind, he thought…I'll walk Valentino, get back and have breakfast, then get on the phone to Rachel with my news. As far as Janic's life went this constituted a plan.

He walked Valentino around his usual route: down the road and into the park that stretched as far as the borders of the town, and which contained a small area of woodland where he could let the dog off his leash, confident that he'd come to no harm. The dog would take himself off chasing squirrels while Janic could rest on a bench and have a quiet smoke. On reaching the woods, Janic leaned down and released the clasp of the lead from Valentino's collar; the dog duly plunged at breakneck speed into the dense area of trees and bushes, just stirring back into life after a harsh, depressing winter that Janic had thought would never end. He walked twenty yards to a bench, sat down, and reached into his jacket pocket for his cigarettes.

Twenty minutes later Valentino hadn't come back and Janic began to feel mildly alarmed. Usually the dog's initial enthusiasm waned as he invariably failed to catch any squirrels, and normally he would have trotted back by now, tail literally between his legs but eager to resume the rest of their journey. Janic rose from the bench and began to walk quickly into the woods, intermittently calling the dog's name.

He was mightily relieved when he heard Valentino's distant barking. He slowed down his pace and tried to modulate his breathing. Now he could see his dog about a hundred yards ahead, standing on the edge of what looked to be a small clearing, his barking becoming more frenetic and accompanied by a low growling. Janic thought that perhaps he'd seen rabbits, or maybe even a deer. As he came up to Valentino he called:

"Hey, what's the matter, boy? What's all that fuss about?"

As Janic looked up at the clearing to see what had bothered Valentino he froze, and the taste of last night's brandy mixed with bile rushed in an acidic swell from his gorge to his throat. He collapsed to his knees, staring in disbelief at what he saw, his mouth agape. The ground was covered with hundreds and hundreds of skulls of all shapes and sizes: men, women and children. In the middle of this grim scene stood an ageing crone, the old woman from his nightmares, beckoning to him with the bony index finger of one scrawny, outstretched arm and smiling a toothless smile.

"Welcome, Janic; welcome to a place of skulls," she croaked harshly. "You have reached your destiny."

He stood up somewhat unsteadily and felt himself drawn inexorably forward, as if he was hypnotized once more. This was a living nightmare, one from which Janic instinctively knew there could be no awakening.

Overhead, in the branches of an oak tree, a crow began to screech; a noise which steadily grew into a deafening, throaty roar.

AIN'T NO GRAVE CAN HOLD MY BODY DOWN

The passing of autumn into winter always depressed Skinnybones. He could remember worse winters in his long life than the relatively mild ones he'd experienced over the last couple of years: long, dark and freezing cold seemingly endless days when human prey was hard to come by and he'd had to rely on killing wild animals such as foxes, rabbits and badgers in order to survive. Days that were always the same, indistinguishable one from another. Bleak black voids that plunged his mood into prolonged bouts of misery. He'd heard humans speaking of something called 'global warming' as being responsible for the change in the seasonal climates; Skinnybones had no idea what that was, but winter still depressed him all the same, mild or harsh. I'm getting old, he thought, too damned old. I'm a survivor, the last of my kind, human flesh has sustained me for centuries. But to what end? What had been the point of it all? Passing away the long lonely days was becoming an increasing struggle. Loneliness; that was the key to it, he thought. I have no offspring to ensure the survival of my species.

He trudged wearily through the woods, over blankets of newly-fallen leaves that crackled and crunched underfoot. Presently he came upon a large lake; he sat by the water's edge and cast his gaze over the flinty, blue-grey expanse in front of him, the breeze rippling the surface seeming to whisper hundreds of hushed secrets in the otherwise complete silence. He thought, maybe it's time to go. He'd ridden his luck for centuries, through all the hue-and-cries against his species from times when humans rode horses and hunted with packs of snarling, baying hounds to the present day, when humans seemed to be too wrapped up in their own worries and concerns to notice anything else. Skinnybones was no philosopher concerning humans; they were merely his primary food source. But their odd, erratic and eccentric behaviour often fascinated him. Killing them sometimes

13

seemed wrong, cruel even. Maybe he was going soft in his old age. He quickly dismissed the thought. No, I need to eat. To survive. To be a survivor. Back to the same question as before, though. Why?

He looked down at the ground around his feet and, finding several small stones, picked a few of them up and sent them skimming across the water. And suddenly a perverse thought struck him: could he mate with a woman-human? Could he, for once, resist the promise of fresh meat and lush warm blood and procreate to produce – what sort of being? It would be a strange hybrid, for sure, but hopefully one with more of his attributes than human ones. Whatever it turned out like, it would have his genes, too. What if the chosen woman-human had more than one child – a male and a female? Ideal. They could mate and produce more like themselves and ensure the continuation of his species, albeit a diluted version. It was the only way. Of course it would mean having to hold the woman captive during her gestation period, then once she'd given birth she would no longer be of use to him. Or perhaps she could; she'd be the offspring's first meal. He grinned. And he would then have a family, something he now realized he wanted more than anything in this world, on this planet. Loneliness was like a black hole in his soul that sucked in all his feelings and emotions. Of course, if he were to carry out his plan it would mean going where the humans lived, places he'd tried to avoid throughout his life since the Great Purges of his people. Tomorrow…he would think more about this tomorrow. But deep down he knew his mind was made up.

Sally Robinson closed her front door and walked slowly back to her kitchen, sighing and shaking her head. What a waste of fucking space he was, she thought. Five minutes of awkward fumbling and groaning and it had all been over. Men were so pathetic. Mind, it had been worth it. She took the roll of notes from the pocket of her dressing gown and shoved them in her bag. She wasn't proud of what she did but she needed the money, it helped her to survive. And wasn't that, after all, what life was about? Making sure that you were able to carry on. It was her body, anyway. She moved across to the sink, filled her kettle, and spooned instant coffee into her mug, which bore the legend: 'Don't panic, just lie back and relax'. Reading that always made her smile.

Taking her drink through to her small front room, she picked up the TV remote and flicked it at the screen. Up came the local news: a reporter was relating the breaking news of a rambler who had been discovered brutally murdered in Donnithorne Woods; his body had been hideously disembowelled and it looked as if large parts of his flesh had been chewed off. It looked like the work of a crazed animal, but the victim's wallet, found nearby, was empty. So robbery seemed to have been the motive. Police would be making a formal statement later, were appealing for witnesses... Behind the reporter, there was a mass of police activity: crime scene tape was strung between trees that flapped madly in the strong breeze, arc lights had been set up to enable a more thorough search of the immediate area around the body in the gathering dusk, and several officers and SOCO's wearing white protective suits were bustling about. Sally switched off the set. Christ, she thought, what's this world coming to? The news had unnerved her, but apart from her obvious shock and horror, she couldn't think why. She needed to get showered and changed soon – her evening shift at the Fox Inn started in an hour's time. She enjoyed the job: the banter, and the prospect of a punter who wanted a bit more than real ale or lager. She switched off the TV and went upstairs to her bathroom.

Skinnybones licked his thin lips after he'd eaten the intestines of his latest victim, a fortuitous kill that had been quite unexpected, a lone walker in the woods he'd been able to despatch and butcher quite quickly. He'd not felt able to eat much, though; felt bloated on what little he had managed to consume. He worried he may be losing his appetite. Another symptom of getting too old, he thought... The stuff he'd taken from his victim's pouch-thing would come in handy, too, when he was able to pluck up the courage to go where humans lived and carry out the plan he was now resolved on. He took the small bundle of folded sheets of paper from the pocket of his long, black cowl, along with a few

15

circular discs and looked at the strange pictures and undecipherable symbols. He knew that humans called this stuff 'money' but he had no idea of its worth or value; what he did know was that he would need it in exchange for things he would need in the town, like food that humans ate (the thought of that made him shudder. But then he remembered that they also ate meat), and a room in which to stay. Perhaps even clothes like they wore, to make him look as inconspicuous as possible. Or maybe not. Any human who questioned his appearance wouldn't be long for this world. But above all it would enable him to survive – there was that word again – in his brief foray into the town. He popped a couple of his victim's fingers into his mouth, chewed gently, enjoying the crack of bones and the tough, sinewy flesh that his still razor sharp teeth tore through with ease. Always room for a couple of fingers…Then, getting up from the fallen tree trunk on which he'd been sitting, he walked to the edge of the woods and looked down the valley at the town that nestled serenely in its palm. Brakedale, he thought. Where my destiny lies. He began the walk towards the faintly glowing orange/yellow lights, a vague feeling of uneasiness beginning to grip the pit of his stomach.

Sally arrived for her shift a good ten minutes before it was due to start. The lounge was completely empty, and the bar contained just a couple of elderly locals who looked up from the domino game they'd been engrossed in and smiled simultaneous greetings. Then quickly looked down again and recommenced their game. Sally moved behind the counter, and lifted a can of polish from one of the shelves with which she intended to clean the brass fittings of the hand-pulled beer pumps. Tonight was going to be a slow night, off-season for tourists and it was Monday, traditionally a quiet night in pubs after the busy weekend. The landlord appeared holding a card of peanuts he'd fetched from the cellar. "Hiya, Sal," he said in greeting.

"Hi Jim. Won't be much going off tonight."

"Nah. Quiet as the grave. Hopefully it might pick up a bit later." He took the empty card down from the wall beside the till and replaced it with the new one, casting a surreptitious, appraising glance at Sally as he did so. At her shoulder length, curled red hair that was pulled back in a ponytail, the bright blue eyes, and the beautifully slender young body that was tonight clothed in tight black jeans, open-necked black shirt and tan coloured suede jacket. He loved her gently lilting, soft Irish accent. He was aware of her 'other career' but was not prejudiced against her. Would love to spend some quality time with her himself but his missus, with her built-in radar, would be sure to find out. Jim himself was in his early sixties, with a mop of steely-grey hair and ruddy outdoor complexion more often associated with Norfolk farmers. Too old for her anyway, he thought. She probably wouldn't want to go with an old fart like me. Sally had class, would surely have high standards. He sighed heavily as the title of a film he'd watched recently popped into his head, seeming quite apt: *No Country for Old Men.*

"You OK, Jim?" Sally asked him.

"Yeah, just thinking about things I can never have," he replied, enigmatically. Sally adopted a confused expression then smiled as the probable meaning of his comment dawned on her.

"I'm just going back down the cellar to change the Theakston's," Jim continued. "Give me a shout if it gets busy." This last comment was said more in gentle sarcasm than any real hope that a coachload of punters would suddenly burst into the bar. Sally turned back to the pumps and began her polishing.

A quarter of an hour later the door opened to admit a tall figure dressed in a black cowl, the hood pulled well forward over his head. He stopped as the door swung shut behind him, then walked with slow, hesitant steps up to the bar where Sally was still polishing. She looked up as the figure approached her and put her duster down, regarding this strange-looking figure that had stopped directly in front of her, looking up and down the row of now brightly-gleaming pumps that sparkled in the light. The figure raised a hand and pointed at one of the pumps. Sally noticed the long, bony fingers and the cracked nails, which had traces of what looked like dried blood beneath them.

"A pint, will it be?" Sally asked.

The figure nodded, his hood still pulled forward so she was unable to see his face. Sally reached for a pint glass and

17

commenced pouring.

"A bit late for Halloween, aren't we?" she said, placing the foaming brown liquid in front of the figure. There was no response, and Sally instantly regretted her comment, feeling that she'd offended the man.

"That'll be two pounds sixty-four, please," she said. The man reached into the pocket of his cowl and pulled out an assortment of coins which he slapped down onto the counter, making no effort to count out the correct amount. A foreigner he must be, Sally thought, unused to our currency. She reached through the pumps and picked up two pound coins, a fifty pence piece, and assorted coppers to make up the rest. She then turned and walked towards the till to ring the money in, beginning to feel slightly uneasy about the stranger's silence. Probably can't speak English either, she reassured herself. When she looked at the bar again the man had taken his glass and moved to a corner table. The two elderly regulars had now left, and Sally was alone in the bar with this man.

Alone with Skinnybones.

George Jones paced in furious strides around the sitting room of his small terraced house, feeling agitation and frustration in equal measure. Christ, but he loved Sally Robinson and would do anything for her. He abruptly ceased his pacing and sat down heavily on his sofa, taking several long, deep breaths in an effort to calm down, tried to think clearly about what he should do. Thoughts of Sally collided in his head. He spent virtually every waking moment thinking about her, her long red hair, the sparkling blue eyes, the gorgeous figure, the way the smile never seemed to leave her lips. He'd first seen her six weeks ago when he was newly arrived in the town and had wanted to get to know the local people, and a visit to the pub seemed a logical place to start. And there she'd been, working behind the bar of the Fox, an angelic vision of indescribable beauty. He'd been instantly smitten. He'd felt instant anger when he'd been told by one of the locals that Sally sold her body for money; telling him, with a sly wink, that he could rent Sally by the hour, if he knew what he meant. The man had noticed the way George kept his gaze firmly focused on Sally, how he'd seemed to be transfixed, mesmerised by her. George had wanted to punch the man's lights out but had managed to resist the urge with a monumental effort; his quickness with his fists and unpredictable temper had got him into a whole heap of trouble before, including with his ex-wife who'd thrown him out of their house, changed the locks and taken out a restraining order against him. Bitch. He hadn't hit her that many times, anyway, just a few reminders to stop talking to other men and laughing at him behind his back.

On subsequent visits to the pub when Sally had been working he'd implored her, begged her to stop prostituting herself. He'd told her he loved her, wanted to marry her and start a family. Sally had merely smiled that far-away smile, saying how could he love her when he didn't know her? He'd replied that he wanted to get to know her, had shouted at her, demanding that she drop those other sad bastards. Sally had seemed to get increasingly annoyed at his persistence, had accused him of wanting to control her life. She'd said that she was a free spirit and no man would ever tell her what she could and couldn't do. Fuelled by large amounts of drink, these comments had infuriated him even further, to the point where last Friday evening that bastard landlord had barred him. Fucker was probably shagging his beloved Sally as well. The thought of that made him feel instantly nauseous. He'd been about to remonstrate with Jim Benson when several of the locals, hearing the increasingly loud commotion, had surrounded him at the bar. Not liking the odds stacked against him, he'd left the pub quietly but with a smouldering resentment and hatred burning his guts.

George reached for the vodka bottle on the coffee table in front of him, poured himself a large measure and took a heavy drink. The liquid had an instantly calming effect. He resolved to go round the pub again later, to have it out with Sally one last time, and make her see the error of her ways. She'd see they would be good for each other, could have a good life together. But if she still wouldn't have him, then no man would have her. Ever again. A broken bottle or glass would see to that.

Skinnybones felt that he was developing a taste for this strange, muddy-brown brew. He'd tasted ale before over his long years, but having never been in a place like this before it had never been served to him in this way, from a pump that must lead to a barrel somewhere. He remembered once when he'd waylaid a monk who'd been leading a donkey through the woods, with two large wooden barrels strapped to either side of the animal's saddle. He'd made a nice meal of the fat priest and, in a rare act of benevolence, had let the donkey wander off into the woods, but not before relieving it of the two barrels. The priest had probably been delivering it to the local inn; perhaps they brewed their own ale in the monastery run by Abbott Bonestaff and sold it to make money. He'd hoisted both barrels effortlessly onto each of his shoulders and had carried them back to the cave he'd been inhabiting at the time. Forcing the stopper from one of them, he'd poured a measure of the liquid into the pewter mug which was amongst the possessions he'd acquired from his human prey. He'd spluttered and coughed at first as he gulped the ale; had then drank more slowly, savouring the taste which seemed both bitter and sweet at the same time. He'd finished off half of one barrel and it had had a strange effect on him; he'd begun to stagger around the cave, seeing double, and finally collapsing into a heavy slumber from which he'd awoken the next morning feeling dreadful. He hadn't touched any more of the drink for days afterwards. Skinnybones smiled at the memory; that had been centuries ago, and his first experience of human drink.

Only two other people had come into the bar since Skinnybones' arrival, and had paid him scant attention, probably taking him to be some sort of monk. Skinnybones smiled at the irony. Perhaps the local people were used to seeing all sorts amongst the tourists to the town and had long since ceased to be curious at their various dress and appearance. They had only stayed for one drink and had soon left, nodding to Skinnybones on their way out and muttering a subdued "good night." Skinnybones hadn't replied. The girl behind the counter with the strange accent he didn't recognize finished polishing glasses with the checked cloth and walked up to his table.

"Will you be wanting another pint, sir? Or perhaps something to eat? We've got rolls with cheese or ham."

Skinnybones pulled back his hood and looked her directly in the eye. Sally gasped in shock, seeing for the first time the heavily lined leathery skin of his face, the beard like the devil's, and those coal-black, liquid eyes that seemed to be gateways into hell itself. She was instantly drawn into them, hypnotized. She stood, unable to move. Then she said: "Or will you be requiring something else entirely?"

Skinnybones pushed his empty glass towards her. It almost slid off the table but just stopped short.

"Just ale, human. Just ale. For now."

Sally walked a bit further forward, still staring into Skinnybones' eyes, and picked up the glass. She wrenched away her gaze and walked back behind the bar as if held in the grip of a powerful spell. She began to pour another beer then jumped with a start as the door suddenly burst open and George Jones staggered into the room. Seeing Sally behind the bar, he walked unsteadily towards her with his arms outstretched.

"Sally, Sally, please listen to me. Please, I beg you. I love you, Sal, you must believe that."

Sally replied in a panicky voice: "Just go, George. Go now or I'll fetch Jim down."

"Oh, and what's that fat twat going to do? Hit me with his rolled up *Daily Telegraph*?"

"George go, you scare me. I'm frightened. I can have the police here in minutes. I don't want any trouble so just get out while you can."

"But Sal…"

A voice from behind George cut him off.

"I think she wants you to go. You would be wise to do as she says."

George turned and noticed the strangely-garbed figure sitting at a table in the corner for the first time. He burst out laughing. "And who the fuck are you, old man? I didn't realize it was fancy dress night," he cackled. Skinnybones rose slowly and walked up to the bar.

"I, human, am your worst nightmare."

"Oh, we'll see about that," George said, still chuckling, and

21

picked up an empty lager bottle left on the bar by one of the previous customers. He held it by the neck and smashed the end down hard on the wooden counter, leaving an ugly mass of razor sharp, jagged green glass. "Come on then, old man, let's see what strength you've got left in that pathetic, skinny body."

Skinnybones calmly reached into the pocket of his cowl and pulled out his blood-stained dagger. Then, with a lightning-fast movement that George saw only as a blur he thrust the weapon at the young man's throat, stopping just short of delivering a fatal blow. He felt the urge to make a kill but resisted, knowing that the last thing he needed was a dead human that would divert him from his main purpose in coming here in the first place.

"Don't make me use this, human. I wouldn't normally hesitate in doing so, believe me."

"OK, OK, calm down, old fella. I was just joking. I'm going, let me go. Get that thing away from me." George dropped the bottle which smashed on the stone floor.

Skinnybones lowered his dagger reluctantly and George Jones, taking one last look at Sally, breathing hard and trembling, walked quickly out of the room, ejected twice now from the same premises in only a couple of days. But he was not finished yet. Not by a long chalk. That skinny old fart wouldn't get the better of him, he thought. How dare he humiliate George Jones in front of his beloved Sally? And he was probably another punter. Someone else who was going to pay to have sex with *his* girlfriend. As he left the pub and breathed in the cold night air in deep draughts, the beginning of a plan began to form in his mind and he slowly began to calm down once more. That bastard won't get the better of me, he thought. And he'll certainly never have Sally. And what the fuck was that bloke anyway? He didn't look human, more like the devil, with that beard. And he had serious dental problems, too, judging by the fangs he'd seen. Fucking freak was in no way human. He began to walk briskly back to his flat, in order to put the first part of his plan into action. He would need to be quick, fearing that by the time he got back the freak would have left the pub with Sally and he'd miss his chance.

Back inside the bar, Sally herself was starting to calm down. She'd been terrified by George's appearance, fearing what he might do. But her – *what*? He was certainly no knight in shining armour – but he had come to her rescue and she was grateful to this odd stranger.

"Like another pint, mister? On me. Thank you for seeing off George."

"A once noble name, too noble for a miserable shit of a human such as him," Skinnybones replied. "Thank you, I find this ale most…gratifying."

"And what's *your* name?" Sally asked.

"I go by the name of Skinnybones. It is not my real name but one given to me by humans in tribute to my skills at butchering flesh."

Sally giggled at the man's strange words and began to refill his glass.

"So, tell me a bit about yourself, Mr Skinnybones," Sally said as she poured. Skinnybones lifted the refilled glass and took a long draught of the deliciously strong ale, wiping the foaming froth from his beard when he'd finished, and put the glass back down on the bar. He was starting to feel slightly woozy. He looked directly at Sally once more; once more she looked into those piercing eyes, black as midnight, that she noticed seemed to reflect no light that bored right into her, holding her transfixed. Skinnybones began his narrative:

"I come from a race of beings who are not human in origin but who have inhabited this planet for thousands of years. Our exact origins are unknown, as we were never a race of record-keepers, archivists or storytellers. We are merely survivors. Centuries ago your king, Avric, known as the Tyrant King during that period you humans refer to as the Dark Ages in your history books when many events transpired that were only vaguely recorded, employed us as hunters to track down and kill those he termed 'Deniers', that is, people opposed to his accession to the throne and his rule which had been achieved at the expense of his brother's life, whom Avric murdered. His brother, Rannard, had been the incumbent king and was a good and benevolent monarch. Avric used us because we were ruthless and because he found his own soldiers employed to hunt Deniers were becoming increasingly unreliable. They became lazy and greedy, plundering money and treasures from their victims and keeping it for themselves. The Tyrant King believed the wealth to be his by right. Many times some of these soldiers, allied together in large groups, having designs on the throne themselves, tried to overthrow Avric. He successfully put down each rebellion by utilizing my people. As I said, we were ruthless. We had no designs on the throne ourselves, merely relished the thrill of the hunt and the taste of human flesh as our reward. The king was highly satisfied with our work and gladly let us devour our prey.

"Then, decades later, things changed when Avric was eventually overthrown by his cousin, Prince Arne. The prince had returned to these lands after many years on crusades throughout lands in the east thousands of miles away. Arne was appalled by the horrors that he returned to, and the evil of Avric's despotic rule. The land was riven with fear and the people were harshly treated and terrorized. The final straw was his discovering of the fact that Avric had murdered his brother in order to usurp the throne. So the prince sent his armies forward to topple Avric and was successful in overthrowing him after only a few battles. Avric was hanged along with his leading generals. Arne assumed the throne and vowed to continue Rannard's good works.

"Next, Arne turned his attention to my people. We had fought loyally and bravely for Avric but our numbers were few and we were soon routed in what the new king termed the Great Purges. Those that were not killed by Arne's soldiers were driven into the surrounding countryside and scattered to the four winds. We survived on whatever human victims we could find, always on the move and in fear of our lives. Over the centuries we continued to be hunted down and our numbers dwindled further, until the present day when I believe that I am the only survivor."

Sally, who'd been smiling broadly throughout Skinnybones' story, shook her head when he'd finished and said: "My God, Mr Skinnybones, you tell one incredible yarn worthy of us Irish. You ought to write it all down, you'd make a great fantasy or horror writer!"

Skinnybones had no idea what the human-woman's words meant exactly; she seemed to be suggesting that he become some sort of scribe. He said: "As I mentioned earlier, my people were no sort of scribes. If I could draw symbols on parchment, then I would make a record of my history."

Sally burst out laughing. "Tell you what, Mr Skinnybones, you can borrow my laptop!" then, fearing that she had upset and offended the stranger, she said, "I'm sorry, Skinnybones. That was unkind of me. Please, have another drink."

"I accept, but this one I will pay for. You seem not to believe my words, woman-human. Why is that?"

"Well, it seems so incredible. Again, I'm sorry."

"It matters nothing to me. You will soon learn the truth of my words."

Skinnybones leaned against the bar as Sally once more replenished his drink. He was fascinated by this red-haired creature. She would make a good mate, a worthy mother of his offspring. A pity her life would be cut short once she'd served her purpose. It must be the effect of this intoxicating drink, but Skinnybones seemed to be warming to this human, experiencing emotions that he'd never felt before.

For her part, Sally felt strangely drawn towards this stranger. Who, or what the hell was he? He was certainly one odd dude. She couldn't take her gaze away from those intense eyes for long; they drew her in like a magnet, hypnotising her. He certainly wasn't anywhere near her usual class of client but...he was interesting, unique, made her laugh with his strange words and stories. And he had money.

Suddenly, Skinnybones jumped in alarm as the jukebox started up on a free-play; Johnny Cash's mournful tones singing 'Ain't No Grave Can Hold My Body Down.' Skinnybones was alarmed; flinched away from the deafening noise.

"What horrible row is that?" he said.

"Guess you're not a Johnny Cash fan then, eh?" Sally replied. She reached for the remote underneath the counter and clicked the jukebox off.

George Jones hunted through the cupboard under his stairs and eventually found what he was looking for; his baseball bat. This'll see to that weird fucker, he thought, running his hand along the smooth, shiny surface. He struggled to think how he'd come by the bat, then remembered it had been a booby prize in a pub quiz. He'd been captain of the team that had come last. He placed the bat inside his leather jacket and zipped it up, but the last third of its length was still visible. No matter. It was dark and it was late and nobody would see him or notice it, he felt sure. He hurriedly left the house and ran back to the pub to await the time when that weird fucker would leave, hoping against hope that he hadn't already done so.

Jim Benson came down to the bar and called to Sally. "You get off, Sal. I don't expect we'll get any more customers now. It's only a matter of half an hour anyway. I'll pay you your full shift, of course. And don't worry about the clearing up, I'll see to that." Then, when he noticed the strange figure dressed in black standing at the bar, he said, "Oh, sorry, sir. Didn't see you there."

"No matter," Skinnybones replied, "I was just about to leave, anyway."

"Wait for me outside. Please," Sally called to Skinnybones. "Give me ten minutes and I'll be with you." Then, turning to Jim, she said, "Thanks. Is it alright if I just pop up and say goodbye to Moira?"

"Of course it is, she'll be pleased to see you."

Jim's wife was recuperating from a severe bout of flu, and she'd taken an instant liking to Sally since she'd started working at the pub, seeing her as the daughter she'd never had. As Sally ascended the stairs at the back of the bar, Jim called out, "Be careful on your way home, Sal. You don't know who's about these days." Then, looking at the back of the strange man who was now walking out of the pub, he repeated, this time in a whisper, "You just don't know who's about," and shook his head sadly.

Skinnybones was feeling distinctly ill. The rush of cold air hit him as he walked out into the night. He stood outside the pub's exit, breathing rapidly. It was ages since he'd drunk ale and was now feeling its full effects. But he felt gratified that he had now obtained his mate, and grinned evilly, imagining the child, or children, he would have in less than a year. It had all been so easy;

26

easier than he had dare think. He'd merely used the hypnotic effect of his eyes which had stood him in good stead with human prey for centuries, stopping them in their tracks. It was a shame, really, about this Sally-thing. She seemed so innocent, had no idea of her fate, of what Skinnybones had planned for her.

He began to pace up and down, impatiently waiting for the woman-human. Most likely due to the large amount of ale he'd consumed, he didn't feel the heavy blow to the back of his skull. His normally razor-sharp senses had been dulled by the alcohol. Skinnybones crumpled to the floor within seconds. Behind him, the tall, powerful figure of George Jones stood, raising his baseball bat aloft again in case another blow was necessary to subdue the weirdo. The figure slumped on the pavement lay motionless, however, so George lowered the weapon. Adrenaline surged through him, he felt charged with electricity; it negated the effects of the large amount of alcohol that he too had drunk. He leaned down and poked the inert figure with the tip of his bat, just to make sure. Still no response. He placed the bat back inside his jacket and leaned forward and down once more, albeit awkwardly this time. The bat was a hindrance, but he managed to haul the strange creature up and sling it over his shoulder. In a previous life George had been a fireman, until he'd been sacked for being drunk on duty and had punched his Duty Officer. So picking people up and carrying them was no problem for him. Besides, there was no weight at all to this thing – whatever it was. He looked about him nervously, adrenaline still pumping, to see if he'd been observed. There was nobody about; the street was completely empty. The streetlights cast their eerie yellow glow as he scanned up and down; there were several lights on behind the curtains in some of the front rooms of the houses, but he was confident that he had not been seen. He hurried forward as quickly as he was able given the burden he was carrying, back towards his house.

Just a few minutes after George had disappeared into the shadows Sally emerged from the pub, shouting a final "Goodnight" to Jim Benson. She, too, scanned the street up and down in search of Skinnybones, but the stranger was nowhere to be seen. She called out, as loudly as she dared, not wanting to disturb the peace, but there was no response. Young or old, she thought, men are shits. Complete and utter shits. She began the walk back home, looking into a few of the alleyways between houses on her way, thinking perhaps the stranger was hiding in one of them ready to pounce on her like in some childish game, but she saw no-one on her short journey.

On reaching his house, George fumbled in his jacket pocket for the door key while balancing his burden on his shoulder. He'd had an awkward moment when he turned into the road and almost cannoned into a dog walker. Thinking quickly, he'd explained to the startled woman, who eyed him suspiciously on regaining her composure, that he was carrying his drunken pal home from the pub so he could crash for the night on his sofa. The woman had turned her gaze to the baseball bat poking out of George's jacket. "It was a rough pub and we were expecting trouble," was the only pathetic explanation he could give. He moved on swiftly past her, relieved when he heard the woman's footsteps receding in the other direction.

Now, he realized, he had a big problem; what to do with the body? He closed the door behind him and threw Skinnybones' body onto the hall floor. George felt sure that he'd killed the old freak; to make absolutely sure he knelt down and placed his fingers on its throat; no pulse. No sign of life whatsoever. An idea came to him. At the rear of the house was a rundown garden that was full of patchy grass, weeds, and an assortment of ancient rusted bicycle frames and prams with no wheels left by previous occupants. And in the top corner was a large, overgrown bramble bush with enough space between it and the bottom fence to dig a grave. Top idea; the grave would be totally unnoticed by his neighbours there, and just as an extra precaution, he'd chuck loads of the assorted rubbish on top. Perfect. Feeling good now that he had a plan, George went to the cupboard in search of his spade.

Sally arrived back at her flat and let herself in, feeling dejected. She walked to her fridge for a bottle of chardonnay and poured herself a glass, then flopped down wearily on her sofa. She couldn't get the stranger out of her head. Skinnybones, indeed. Perhaps it *was* only a nickname. It had been those eyes, though. Those eyes that had been so black and intense, beckoning her, drawing her into their depths. But there had been no light there, nothing to indicate anything of the man's nature or character. Lifeless eyes. A cold shiver ran down her spine. She remembered what she'd thought about him in the pub; he had indeed been unique and interesting, and he certainly had a way with a story. She hadn't studied the Dark Ages in history at school and so couldn't verify what he'd told her but it had sounded a brutal and terrifying period. She had Google on her phone and would check it out later. Perhaps tomorrow. She couldn't be fussed with it now.

Sally felt grateful to the stranger for leaping to her defence when George approached her. A real gentlemanly thing to do that had been. She'd felt safe with him being there to protect her. But that knife he carried – surely that was illegal? And what the hell did he use it for? There had been what looked to be traces of dried blood on its blade. Again, she shivered. Perhaps he was a homicidal maniac who had – what? Come to her aid when she'd been threatened by that drunken arsehole George? It just didn't make sense. The man had been a mystery, a total enigma. But overall, she'd liked him. And then he'd just disappeared, not waited for her like he said he would. So, another time-waster like the rest of them. And then she remembered that he hadn't actually said that he *would* wait for her. She'd just assumed that he would. No man had ever turned her down before, professionally, so to speak, or otherwise.

She took a swig of her wine and sighed heavily when she thought of George Jones. There was a bomb waiting to go off, for sure. How could he have become so obsessed with her in so short a time? He'd only been to the pub a few times, being new to the area. He'd seemed friendly at first and…well…normal, but she'd soon noticed that the more he drank the more his eyes bored into her; it had felt like a physical force. That had soon morphed into the old common-or-garden lecherous drooling. And telling her who she could and couldn't see, what she couldn't do, what was that all about? Creepy, obsessive, jealous bastard. Her anger was beginning to flare and she began to tremble. She tipped what was left of the wine into her glass and took another drink. Perhaps it would be best if she went round to see George and nipped the trouble right in the bud before it got out of hand. Tell him in no uncertain terms where he stood, which was nowhere with her. George had told her where he lived during one of their chats in the pub while she was working. Yes, she would go round tomorrow night, before she went on shift. But would she be safe? She had a sudden idea to text her sister and let her know where she was going, and what time she would arrive there. And if she didn't receive another text exactly half an hour later she should phone the police. At times like this Sally wished she had a big, fierce dog to protect her.

She felt as if she were about to burst into tears of helplessness. But it was just the drink. And she giggled lightly when she thought of what else she had to do tomorrow. Google that Avric bloke. And what were those other names he'd mentioned? One had been Bone something…yes, Bonestaff, that was it. Abbott Bonestaff. So many references to bones…Bonestaff, Skinnybones, and someone called Rannard. She finished her drink and decided it was time for bed. Trudging up the stairs, she thought that going round to see George tomorrow and have it out with him might be a crazy idea but what else could she do? She would sleep on it, and resolved that if she could think of a better idea in the meantime then she would give it a lot of deep thought. She hated confrontation, had always shied away from it. But sometimes it was the only way. Oh, where was her mysterious stranger when she needed him?

After twenty minutes of steady digging George had a man-sized hole. Not the regulation six feet in depth but that hardly mattered; what he had was deep enough to conceal a body. He'd had to be as quiet as possible, of course, so as not to rouse the suspicions of his neighbours. Last thing he needed was the curtain-twitching brigade poking their noses into his business. But all was quiet, all was serene. He looked at his watch: 11.40pm. Most of his neighbours would be in bed by now, anyway, deep in the land of dreams. He could see no lights in either the upstairs or downstairs windows of the houses around him. He felt relieved that his luck was holding out.

Walking back into his house, he saw the still inert body on the hall floor. Didn't get the better of George Jones, did you, he thought, and grinned. You piece of absolute shit, how dare you assume that my girl would go with you. Freak. He kicked Skinnybones and began to laugh. "I'd tip petrol on you and set you on fire and watch you burn if I could do it without attracting attention," he screamed at the body; then cupped his hands hastily over his mouth. The walls of these houses were paper-thin. But as he listened intently for a full minute, he heard no sound.

He grabbed its legs and began to drag the body towards the kitchen door. As he did so, one of the leather moccasins fell off, revealing long, tapered toes and filthy, sharp toenails. "Christ," George said, being careful to whisper this time, "you need to see a fucking podiatrist as well as a dentist." He laughed at his own humour, and picked up the moccasin and placed on top of the body, and continued dragging. Once outside, he had another quick look around for any signs of life; still none were evident. He pulled and heaved Skinnybones over the rough ground, soon reaching the bramble bush and his freshly-dug grave, where he unceremoniously tipped Skinnybones in. The body gave a muffled thud as it hit the bottom. He picked up his spade once more and began to cover the body with earth. When he'd finished, he walked over to the rusty frame of an old kid's bicycle, picked it up, and returned to the grave where he pushed it down on top of the soil, making it look as best he could as if it had been there for ages. For good measure he picked up several rocks and threw those on too. "There's your fucking headstone and a few ornaments," George whispered. "Just don't expect any fucking flowers."

Picking up his spade, he walked as quietly as he could back into the house. He needed a drink after his evening's labours. He felt exhausted.

Sally slept fitfully, her strange dreams populated with images of men on horseback hunting down people who were trying desperately to escape their pursuers in fear and terror. She woke up suddenly with a scream; the last image she'd seen had been of one of these hapless people, who looked like ordinary villagers dressed in peasant garb, being decapitated as a sword came arcing down, slicing off their head, which had rolled away into a ditch. The dream had turned quickly into a full-blown nightmare. Sally was panting hard and sweating profusely. She picked up her glass of water from the bedside table and took a long gulp, spilling a large amount of the liquid on her duvet as her hands were shaking so badly. She looked at the luminous green numbers of her bedside alarm clock: 4.35am. She realized that it would be pointless trying to get back to sleep again; besides, she didn't want any more nightmares like those she'd just had. She switched on her bedside lamp and rose out of bed. She needed good, strong tea. And aspirin; her head was pounding like there was something inside her skull trying to hammer its way out.

George Jones had slept heavily, thanks mostly to the large quantity of drink he'd consumed throughout the previous evening. He got up and pulled open his bedroom curtains; the view he had was of the rear of his house, so he was able to see the bramble bush, if not the newly-dug grave that lay just behind it. Nothing looked to have been disturbed. The early morning was grey and overcast, there was no sunshine and the prospect of another gloomy, lonely day lay ahead. As he stood looking out of the window, a pitch-black crow suddenly landed near the bramble bush and began cawing frantically. Soon it was joined by another, and then a third, all making one hell of a cacophony. He closed the curtains again and stepped away, feeling slightly unnerved by what he'd seen.

George thought about his dreams. They had been of strange figures clad in black digging up graves and exhuming bodies. Crazy to think that that could happen in his waking world but the effects of the vodka were making him feel extremely nervous and edgy. He didn't feel too hung over, though, and decided a full English breakfast was in order. This instantly cheered his mood, but he became depressed again when he thought of Sally. Killing the freak wasn't a problem, he hadn't looked local and besides even if he was no-one would be able to make a connection between them. George hadn't threatened to kill him and as far as anyone was aware the black-clad stranger had just walked away into the night. No, the problem was what to do about Sally. Going to the pub again wasn't an option; although her new protector was no longer around to defend her with his strange butcher's knife there was still Jim Benson to contend with. He needed a plan. He would make his breakfast, get some fresh air with a walk down to the shop for some milk and a paper, and spend the rest of the day thinking about what he would do to win Sally over. Before he left the bedroom, he looked proudly up at the display board screwed to the wall, on which were pinned dozens of photographs that he'd secretly taken; all of Sally Robinson. Sally entering and exiting the local supermarket, ditto the local gym. Snaps he'd taken of her walking in the park on a Sunday afternoon, even one he'd taken of her in the pub on his phone as she'd been working, bending down filling a shelf with clean glasses. She hadn't seen or suspected a thing. His eye caught the solitary picture he'd taken a week or so ago of her walking towards her house with a middle-aged man he didn't know or care to know. A 'client', he'd suspected. George had burned the man's eyes out with a cigarette and stabbed several holes into his body with a kitchen knife so that even his mother wouldn't have recognized him. He'd then scrawled 'I love you, there can be no other', followed with a small red heart symbol in blood-red felt pen at the bottom of the image. He turned away and walked downstairs.

Entering his kitchen, George walked up to the window blinds and pulled up the cord. This view also looked out onto his back garden. He saw that the crow had been joined by a half-dozen more, all of them cawing like an insane choir. The noise was growing louder and louder. Christ, he thought, this is becoming like a scene from that Hitchcock film. He unlocked the back door and stepped out into the garden, and walked towards the bramble bush, the grave and the crows. When he had a view of the grave, he saw that two more crows had perched on the bicycle frame at its head and were contributing to the racket. They displayed no fear at George's approach, but rather seemed to turn towards him and stare, continuing with that God awful noise. He suddenly felt completely freaked out. He ran towards the birds, clapping his hands loudly, shooing them away. They took off, as if at one command, and silence at last prevailed as the sounds trailed away. When he looked down at the grave, he noticed several dozen scratch marks in the soil, as if one or more of the birds had been digging with their claws, and also several small, deep holes that looked to have been jabbed with their beaks.

Christ, he thought, they were trying to dig the fucker out.

Sally had spent a good hour of the morning on the phone to her sister, Kate. She'd originally planned to text Kate with her intentions that evening concerning George, but on reflection she felt that her sister deserved a fuller explanation. Kate had instantly become worried and had tried to talk Sally out of it. They had reached what they both thought of as a common sense compromise; Kate would drive over to Sally's flat in the afternoon and they would have a good long girly chat, then go round and tackle the weirdo stalker together. Sally felt encouraged by this; her elder sister, who knew all about what George had been putting her through, was a black belt in karate and would certainly have her uses if the proverbial push came to shove. Kate didn't approve of Sally's alternative income stream but loved her sister deeply. The feeling from Sally was mutual. Kate might not approve of what Sally did, but she didn't judge her. They agreed on a rendezvous time of 3pm, as Sally was on an earlier shift at the pub commencing at 5pm. That would give them plenty of time for their chat and then to go and deal with George Fucking Jones.

George had spent most of the day in a state of nervous agitation. He'd been unable to concentrate on his current book or on the crossword in his daily paper. The large amount of caffeine that he was drinking certainly wasn't helping, so he took the vodka bottle from his kitchen table along with last night's unwashed glass and moved into his front room. The muscles in his left jaw were twitching uncontrollably as he poured himself a drink. The crows had returned to his garden several times during the morning and had been trying to resume their work. The noise they had made had become deafening, drilling into his skull like a pneumatic drill. He'd had to run out into the garden as before to shoo them away. But not long after he had done this, they had returned. All was quiet for the moment, though; perhaps they'd given up. And the really worrying thing was that his neighbours had noticed, had come out to investigate the noise and had witnessed George's odd behaviour. That would take some explaining, but fuck it, it could wait. But he knew that the body would have to be dug up and moved elsewhere, somewhere out in Donnithorne Woods, perhaps. There, those fucking birds could screech away all they liked, he wouldn't care. Within no time at all the corpse would be rotted and would soon be a distant memory. He thought about what, if any, significance there was in the crows' crowding around and digging of the grave. Crows were associated with death and evil, weren't they? He'd Google it later, at a time when he could hopefully see his laptop screen clearly. So, if that were true, who, or what exactly, was that thing he'd killed? Dressed in black and with that beard and those fangs, the weirdo had certainly looked demonic. And that knife he'd brandished, that he'd held at his throat, he'd noticed what looked like dried blood on eat. As the alcohol mixed with the caffeine, George began to have severe misgivings about what he'd done. Outside, at the back of the house, he could hear the deafening crow's choir start up once more. It seemed to be louder than before, becoming more insistent. He took a huge swig of drink and lay back on the sofa, covering his ears with his hands. As he lay there, a random thought came into his befuddled brain; he remembered the collective noun for crows: a *murder*. A murder of crows was gathering once more in his back garden.

"So, Sis, tell me first about this mysterious dark stranger."
　　Kate had arrived at Sally's flat ten minutes earlier and they were both now sitting in the kitchen, nursing mugs of steaming hot coffee. Kate was two years older than her sister; hair a deep

chestnut brown rather than the red of Sally's, eyes of deep blue, and she also spoke in a soft voice that sounded like a light breeze susurrating over a gently rippling lake.

"He came into the pub last night," Sally replied. "I got the impression he was not from around here, but he never exactly said where he was from. Or what his real name was. He just said people had started calling him 'Skinnybones' many, many years ago. He looked distinctly odd – by which I mean, he looked very old, but there was no grey in his hair, or beard that looked like the devil's own. And he looked like he'd had some sort of bizarre cosmetic dentistry at some point. Kate, he had *fangs*, for Christ's sake! But ach, it was his eyes; they pulled you in. It was like being drawn into a long, dark tunnel. I've never seen eyes like that before, on anyone. They didn't look human. Don't laugh, but he reminded me of Dracula. He told me he belonged to a race of people that had lived on Earth for thousands of years but who had no written records of who they were or where they were from. It was all... anecdotal. And even the anecdotal evidence was sketchy, lost through the mists of time."

Sally adopted a far-away expression, looking out of the kitchen window as she'd been speaking. Kate, who had been smiling broadly throughout her sister's narrative, said:

"And was there not something about a story of long-ago kings and a bloody reign of terror? What was that all about? I know we're Irish but we did some English history at school."

"I meant to Google it but didn't get round to it. He referred to the Dark Ages, that period of English history where many things happened that were never properly recorded. It sounds like a time of great uncertainty and upheaval. But how the fuck could anyone be that old?"

There was a pause of several moments where they both took sips of their drinks. Then Kate said:

"It sounds like he really got to you, sis. But he sounds to me like a total fantasist."

"He did get to me, Kate. He did indeed. And perhaps he was – is a fantasist. Whatever. But I was mesmerised by him, and fascinated by his appearance and his stories. But above all else, I felt safe with him when George burst into the pub and started ranting at me, telling me he loved me and shit. He had some sort of knife, and I'm sure he would have used it; he said to George that normally he wouldn't hesitate in doing so. But I'm glad he didn't. Despite everything I didn't want any violence. But he looked like he could handle himself. And that was the other thing that startled me. For someone who reckoned he was so bloody old he could certainly move swiftly enough!"

Both sisters chuckled at this. Then Kate said: "Would you have gone with him, Sal? You know how I mean."

Sally looked at the floor and was silent for a few moments, then she looked up straight into her sister's eyes. "I don't know, Kate. Really I don't. Way too old, not my normal client age range but... as I said, he fascinated me. Perhaps we could have just talked more. Here in my flat. I would have loved that, to hear more of his amazing stories. From a practical point of view, he certainly had money, although he didn't know the value of the notes and coins. I had to count the money out that he offered me to pay for his drinks. So how could he have been English?"

"Sis, you really should be wary and more careful of strangers. You never know who's about. An old cliché, but it's true. I worry about you, and you know how I feel about that side of your life. Sorry, lecture over."

"I know, I know. Point taken. And I really will stop. As soon as I've got enough money together I've decided to go back to Ireland."

"Not to run away from George Jones, I hope? I'll deal with that pathetic little shit."

"No, I made my mind up ages ago, long before he arrived on the scene. Kate, there's nothing for me here. You're OK, you've got your thriving physiotherapy business. You were always the clever one. How are things going, by the way?"

"Fine, just fine. Anyway, back to Mr Jones. Is it not time we went and had our little chat with him?"

Kate had always felt the need to be her little sister's protector. Having herself been the victim of domestic violence three years ago at the hands of a jealous and possessive boyfriend, she knew all about the way some men behaved towards women. It was why she'd taken up karate after suffering six months of abuse. She would never suffer like that again. She glanced at her watch. It was nearly 3.30.

"Christ, what is it about us two, Kate?" Sally said, suddenly sounding wistful and looking out of the window once more. "We always seem to attract the wrong sort."

"It's nothing that we're doing wrong, Sal, you must believe that. It's just the way that some men are. Some, but not all. Thankfully they're a minority. Anyway, c'mon. We'll get this over with then I'll drive you to the pub in time for the start of your shift. I'll keep you company for an hour or so. Not that I'm scared of George Fucking Jones but I feel I may need a good stiff drink afterwards."

George was vaguely aware of a heavy banging sound on the periphery of his consciousness. He'd drunk several more vodkas in an attempt to drown out the hellish racket outside in his garden and was just about to lapse into another deep slumber when he heard the insistent thumping on his front door. Confused, he thought that it was one of his neighbours come to complain about the row. He got unsteadily to his feet and walked towards the door, preparing himself for a slanging match with some interfering busybody. When he opened up, he was totally shocked by who he saw. A fierce looking young woman with eyes ablaze with fury, and behind her, his beloved Sally.

"We need to talk, Mr Smith. NOW!" the woman he didn't recognize shouted in his face. Not waiting to be invited in, she stormed into the house, followed by a timid Sally who had an almost apologetic look on her face. George closed the door and followed the girls into his front room.

"Ladies, ladies, what's this all about?" George said. Then, looking at Sally, he said, "Oh, Sal, you look beautiful. This is a total surprise, but I knew you'd see sense. Follow your heart, is what I've always believed."

They all stood in the middle of the living room, making no attempt to sit down. Kate didn't intend this to be a cosy, friendly, little chat. She said:

"Firstly, let me introduce myself. My name is Kate Robinson, Sally's sister. What I have to say is quite plain and simple, George, so that even a Neanderthal slug like you will understand. You will leave Sally alone. That is not a request, it's an order. She is not interested in you, never will be. You're a low-down stinking creep. Can I elucidate any part of that statement to make it any clearer for you?"

George was taken aback by Kate's vitriol. This was surreal, must surely be a dream. No, more like a nightmare. For the first time in his life he was speechless; just stood there, mouth working like that of a goldfish, struggling to find something to say. His temples were pounding and he felt like an utter bag of shit. Several seconds of silence passed, during which Kate glared at George with pure evil in her eyes. Then, almost in a whisper but still with an expression of smouldering hatred, she said:

"Looks like I've succeeded in getting through to you, Mr Jones, judging by your lack of response. Now, I know who you are, what you look like, and where you fucking live. If you come within half a mile of my sister again I swear to God I'll come round here and cut your fucking bollocks off."

Suddenly, a quiet voice spoke to them from the door that led to the kitchen. Although it had a calm tone, there was a distinctive, underlying tone of malevolence:

"That is what I would call sound advice, human. I'm not sure what 'bollocks' are but it sounds like this woman-human is skilled with a knife. A talent I highly appreciate and approve of."

The tall figure wearing a black cowl walked fully into the room. Kate, Sally and George turned round and stared in disbelief. Then Sally shouted:

"Skinnybones!"

For it was he. Large as life and despite his calm demeanour very, very angry.

Sally moved forward as if to hug him, but stopped herself short of doing so, feeling confused as to why he was here but at the same time hugely glad that he was. But it was his expression of sheer hatred that ultimately halted her in her tracks. Then Kate said, slowly shaking her head in disbelief:

"What the fuck is that? Sally, come away now!"

Sally turned back to her sister, and said:

"But this is Mr Skinnybones, Kate. The man I was telling you about. The man from the pub last night."

Through all this, George had turned a ghastly shade of white, but managed to splutter out:

"But I killed you, freak. I fucking killed and buried you. How…? You had no pulse. I checked it."

Skinnybones turned his full attention on George. Then, in a voice that could chill a heated room, he said:

"I have no pulse, human, quite simply because I have no heart. Although I've eaten a few in my time. They taste best whilst they're still beating, by the way."

"Those crows," George croaked, "those crows… got you out of the hole?"

"My little corvid friends certainly helped, yes. They were worried about me. They wanted to make sure I was OK. As you can see, I most certainly am. You had a lucky strike, human, but it will be the last one you ever have."

With these words, Skinnybones sprang forward like a leopard and pulled the knife from the pocket of his cowl. George didn't see what was coming; was only vaguely aware, seeing it in slow motion, of the arc of Skinnybones' arm and then a blisteringly sharp pain in his throat. He staggered backwards, grasping the wound with his right hand, as his blood sprayed in a jet through his fingers. He collapsed onto his knees, gurgling helplessly, gasping for breath, clutching at the wound now with both hands in a futile attempt to stop the massive blood loss. After a few more seconds he flopped completely over onto the floor; he twitched violently a couple of times, and then his breathing stopped altogether.

Skinnybones crouched over the inert body.

"I believe you humans have an expression," he said. "Never start what you can't finish."

He then sprang athletically to his feet and turned his attention to Kate and Sally. Kate was hugging her sister in a tight grip; both were completely rooted to the spot and had expressions of sheer terror. Sally was whimpering helplessly, tears welling in her eyes.

"Holy Mother of God," Kate mumbled, "this is not fucking happening. No way, no how." She wished she had her crucifix and rosary with her. Looking Skinnybones straight into his coal-black eyes, she said:

"Stay away, demon. Don't come any closer. I am fully able to protect my sister and myself."

"I'm sure you are, woman-human," Skinnybones replied casually, "even without recourse to that god you pray to."

He then felt suddenly weary, as if drained of all energy. He turned around and sat down heavily in the nearest armchair, sinking his head into his hands. After a few seconds, he looked up and said simply:

"Go. Get out of here, both of you. Before I change my mind."

He then took a deep breath and exhaled slowly, repeating:

"Go."

Sally broke free of her sister's grip and moved a little way towards Skinnybones.

"What will you do, Mr Skinnybones? Where will you go?"

Skinnybones grunted dismissively.

"I'm tired of living, woman-human. Tired of killing. I am of ancient times, times long past. I no longer belong in this world. I will go back to my beloved forest. For the present. Now get out of my sight, and leave me be."

Sally made an attempt to take a further step forward, but Kate grabbed her tightly by the arm to restrain her.

"Come on, Sal. Let's get out of here. We've seen enough tonight," she said.

Then, leading her sister forward, they both left the room, giving Skinnybones a wide berth.

When he heard the front door close, Skinnybones went over to where George Jones lay, and picked him up, slinging the body over his shoulder. He carried it through into the kitchen, out into the garden, and threw it unceremoniously into the shallow grave that had been meant for him. He then hopped casually over the back fence and began walking towards the woods, thinking as he went about the lost opportunity to mate and have offspring. But deep down he felt that it was never meant to be, that his death would be the end of the line. The end of his species. These thoughts didn't make him feel gloomy or depressed, but rather, in a strange way, relieved. As he reached the edge of the woods, he looked back down the valley at the faintly glowing lights of the town, and something that vaguely resembled a smile animated his lips. Then he turned, and walked back into his shelter, his sanctuary, as rain began to fall. He remembered the last words the Tyrant King ever spoke to him:

"We must survive, Skinnybones. We must survive at all costs."

Perhaps, Skinnybones thought. But you could only survive for so long.

ALMOST HUMAN

"C'mon, Tyler, make a bloody move, will you?"

It was the third time in twenty minutes that Chester had uttered the same words.

"There's no money riding on this game, you know. Man's got time to grow a beard waiting for you to decide."

"Shut the fuck up, Chester. I'm thinking."

"That must really hurt."

Chester sprawled back in his chair, arms slung over the wooden back, and let out a long sigh of impatience. Then let out a fart of the silent-but-deadly variety.

"Christ, Chester, what you been eating? Horse shit?"

Tyler attempted to waft away the smell with his left hand while his right tentatively reached for his one remaining bishop.

"Wouldn't go there if I were you, Tyler. Mate in three moves."

Chester instantly regretted warning Tyler off that particular move: not only because he'd jeopardized his chances of winning the game but he also had the feeling it would take his friend another twenty minutes to decide where to go.

"Aw shit, I quit anyway," Tyler responded, knocking his king over. "I'm pig-sick of this game. Fancy another coffee?"

"Certainly do, my old friend. And a fag." Chester reached into his jacket pocket and pulled out his tobacco tin: began the process of rolling his fifth of that morning.

"Got one for me?" Tyler enquired. Chester handed him the one he'd finished and started the process again. As he did so, Tyler looked up and stared down the street.

"Here she comes, right on time. The Queen Bee."

Coming into view and jogging towards where the two men sat outside the café at their usual table was a vision of singular beauty. Blonde hair tied back in a ponytail, wearing black leggings and a yellow tracksuit top over a lithe, athletic body, Janine Garvey was pursuing her usual Saturday morning circuit of the town. When she reached the two elderly men, she stopped, bent over, placing her hands on her knees. Then she got up, and stretched her arms

43

as far as she could above her head.

"Morning, boys," she said. "Who's winning?"

"Tyler here threw a hissy fit and quit the game," Chester responded. "That's two games to nil to me this morning."

Tyler chuckled at his friend's words, shaking his head, letting Chester enjoy his moment of glory. He'd have his revenge soon enough when, or if, he could be bothered to resume playing. He looked at Janine and said:

"You know, Janine, if I were thirty years younger I'd be jogging right along after you."

"And I'd be slowing down to let you catch up," Janine replied, giving him a cheeky wink, which stirred something fleetingly and half-remembered in Tyler's crotch. His face went a bright shade of red under his grizzled white beard.

"Sit down, Janine, you're making me feel dizzy. It's too damned hot for all that running around," Chester said. Although the girl's arm-stretching exercises had finished she'd begun jogging on the spot, a process that made her perfectly-sculpted breasts jiggle tantalizingly.

"OK, it *is* a bit on the warm side today and I could just do with one of Marlon's excellent Cappuccinos." She plumped herself down in one of the two vacant chairs at the table.

Tyler leaned toward and shouted through the open door of the café.

"Two more for us old farts and a Cappuccino for the lady, Marlon my good man," he bellowed, a throaty roar that could shatter thick ice in winter. Inside, Marlon put down his newspaper and walked back behind his counter with a grunt.

"Could you eat a bun with that fancy Italian stuff, girl?" Tyler asked.

"Hell, why not. I'll jog off the calories later."

The three of them had sat in a companionable silence for several minutes, sipping their drinks, when Janine started to fan the air in front of her face.

"Gosh, it's getting warmer," she said, and began to remove her tracksuit top. It was halfway down her bare arms when she

44

suddenly pulled it back over her T-shirt.

"Second thoughts, best keep it on, I'll be going soon."

Both men instantly picked up on the nervousness in her voice, as if she was making a hasty excuse for something. She began awkwardly trying to fasten the tracksuit's zip, but her shaking fingers were making a laborious job of it. Tyler, who was sitting closest to Janine, had also noticed something about her that caused him to cough and stare at Janine in stunned disbelief. He looked hurriedly away, shaking his head. It was clear that whatever he had seen, Chester had not. Chester seemed to put her manner down to the girl not wanting to show off her bare skin even to these two harmless old buffers. Fair enough, some girls were sensitive about that kind of thing.

"You OK old buddy?" Chester asked.

"Erm… yeah, sure… burned my tongue on coffee, that's all."

Janine seemed to have regained her composure.

"Well, boys, thanks for the sustenance. Best go now – I'm meeting Geoff at twelve."

Tyler and Chester nodded in unison, both saddened that the young girl had to go so soon. It was good to have young company, especially that of a beautiful girl. But Geoff, her brother – she had no boyfriend that either men knew about – would be whisking his sister away somewhere nice for a pub lunch. It was like the young could only take the company of the elderly for so long before getting bored – but hell, life went on. She needed to be around folk her own age.

Janine stood to leave. With old-fashioned manners, that she was deeply touched by, both men rose too.

"Look after yourself, girl" Tyler said.

"Bye, Janine. See you soon," Chester added. "Perhaps you could stop by again next Saturday?"

"Perhaps I could," she replied, and gave another of those cheeky winks. She planted a quick kiss on both men's cheeks, then began to jog back in the direction in which she'd come. Tyler and Chester watched her go until she was a tiny figure that took a left turn and disappeared around a side-street off the town's main road.

"OK, old mate, spill. Something definitely freaked you out back there when Janine began to take her jacket off. What the hell was it? And don't give me that burned-my-mouth-on-coffee shit again. Our drinks were only lukewarm by then."

This from Chester in the bar of the Town Tavern. They'd decided on a pub lunch of their own, and now sat in a quiet corner sipping their pints of real ale. There were no other customers as yet and the barman was changing a barrel in the cellar. It was several seconds before his friend replied. When he did, he switched his gaze from the middle distance to look Chester full in the face.

"Well, it's the weirdest thing I ever saw. There was a patch of skin on her right arm that was different... hell, Chester, it was green. And scaly, like a lizard. I swear."

"Geoff, I think... I think I messed up, big style... I was having coffee with Mr Tyler and Mr Chester... and I began to take my tracksuit top off... and Mr Tyler, I think he saw my skin..."

These words were spluttered out quickly and breathlessly by Janine to her brother on her return to the flat they shared in a quiet suburb of the town.

"Shit, Janine, I told you to be careful. You know how the elderly love to gossip. It'll be all over the town in minutes... we may have to leave here." There was a sudden look of panic on Geoff's face.

Janine, having regained her breath, replied: "No, not those two. I'm certain they won't say anything to anyone... they're not like that. Besides, if more people find out I don't care, I'm sick of being driven out of one town after another. I feel like a bloody fugitive. It's nice here, I feel settled for the first time in years."

Geoff nodded sagely at his sister's words, and then said: "OK. Here we stay. I'm tired of running too, truth be told. If we can accept who and what we are other people should be able to as well."

46

Janine smiled. She could always wrap her brother round her little finger.

Chester was trying to digest what Tyler had told him. He took a long swig of beer and then said:

"You know as well as I do that such beings exist. Those dreadful experiments, years ago…"

"Sure I know… but Janine? She's…" Tyler hesitated, trying to find the right words but not at all sure what he meant.

Chester shook his head, smiling, then continued:

"Her age would be about right… hell, was it really thirty years ago? I remember when that story broke… the scandal it caused, the justified moral outrage. I was still a teacher back then, of course. The staff room was electrified by the news for weeks, it was all anyone could talk about. Nothing short of all-out nuclear war would have changed the subject. Do you remember much about it?"

Tyler was silent for a few seconds, then said, looking up from the table:

"Yep, sure do… I remember the endless number of 'spokesmen' that private laboratory trotted out to try to justify what they'd done. Everyone in their PR department must have had a turn. It seemed to be a different one each time: on the radio, TV… but how could they possibly have justified *that*? Taking chameleon DNA and injecting it into the unborn, merely weeks-old foetuses of those poor pregnant women volunteers – who put themselves forward to earn the pittance in remuneration that was on offer. And fuck knows what other things they did. All in the name of… shit, what *was* their justification?"

"They claimed it would have benefits for the military," Chester said. "Camouflage. You know how chameleons can change their skin colour. They can blend in with whatever environment they're in. So imagine: trying to fight an enemy you can't see. Also it can be a form of thermoregulation – they can turn lighter colours to reflect light during the heat of the day. Ideal for desert combat."

"Remind me what you taught again, Chester?"

47

"Biology! You know that, Tyler. We met shortly after all this blew up – at that conference. You'd just published your first book on the entomology of Madagascar."

"Just teasing. But seriously – I remember the shit it caused the government; brought it down like a house of sand when the tide of discovery swept in. Not one of those bastards was prosecuted, though; even though it was suspected that the lab was doing their dirty work. All the evidence and paper trails mysteriously disappeared."

"You talk of 'the tide of discovery'. That would be the whistle-blower then; the mysterious Mr X," Chester said. "And they never found out who *he* was, either."

Both men lapsed into a silence that lasted for several minutes. They were both thinking the same thing but it was Chester who eventually articulated it:

"And what became of those children born with that shit in their blood? There were dozens of them. They just mysteriously vanished. The whole thing was covered up. But just occasionally one of them shows up – usually in the newspapers reporting when they've been hounded out of whichever town they've tried to make a life in, trying to be as human as possible. Guess I mean *as normal* as possible."

"But they must have been adopted by someone while still kids," Tyler added. "They couldn't have raised themselves. Whoever these people are must have kept quiet about it for thirty years."

Then Chester added: "Of course, you know what this means?"

Tyler shook his head, so Chester continued:

"If Janine is a humeleon, then so is her brother."

Tyler nodded, the penny having now dropped.

"Yeah, I guess so. That hadn't occurred to me. It seems funny hearing that word humeleon again. Haven't heard that expression in a long, long time."

Tyler hadn't been the only one to notice – albeit briefly – the flash of green, scaly skin on Janine's arm. Marlon, the café owner, had been outside clearing a table (a good cover for earwigging other peoples' conversations) when he'd looked up just as the young woman was beginning to remove her tracksuit top. He was shocked to his core by what he'd seen. Surely that lovely girl, whom he'd appraised lovingly on the few times he'd seen her either jogging past or stopping to talk to the two old men, couldn't possibly be one of those... he couldn't think of the word. Humiliations, or something. He hadn't read any reports of sightings of them in the *Daily Sentinel* for many, many years. And then one turns up on his doorstep... well, he wasn't going to tolerate one of those filthy freaks being anywhere near his premises, beautiful or not. They were dirty and carried tropical diseases, half of which had no known cure. It said so in the *Sentinel*. When Tyler and Chester had gone, he'd walked quickly outside to the table where they'd been sitting and picked up all four chairs, which he carried through the café to the yard at the rear, and then gone back for the table. He'd burn them later. He didn't want to destroy good, expensive furniture but he had the health of his other customers to think of. He then walked to the sink and washed his hands thoroughly under the hot water tap, standing it for as long as he could before it began to scald his skin. He applied half a bottle of antibacterial liquid soap, and having dried his hands he repeated the process using up the remaining soap. I'm not having one of those creatures in my café, or in my town, he thought, and walked to his phone and quickly jabbed out a number.

The following Saturday Tyler and Chester were at their usual table outside Marlon's, chessboard set out between them but neither man in any mood to start the game. They'd met a couple of times during the week and talk had drifted towards Janine and Geoff and their fears for them should their secret become known by the wider public. It was Tyler who broke the silence.

"Specism is a dreadful thing. Right up there with racism. How could folk be so cruel to the poor victims of those dreadful experiments? It was hardly their fault. They're often driven out of every town they're discovered in, and treated as second-class citizens if they're not and graciously permitted to stay. It's

49

shocking, truly fucking shocking."

Chester nodded his head.

"I totally agree. I heard of a case a couple of years back where the children of a human and humeleon couple – neither kid had any chameleon characteristics, which can happen – were beaten to within an inch of their lives by other kids. And the teachers stood by and watched them do it. No action was taken. Specism is supposed to be a crime but the police rarely prosecute. If ever. They're just as corrupt as the politicians."

Neither Tyler nor Chester had taken much notice of the sharply-dressed young man seated at the table next to them, who was leafing through a copy of the weekend edition of the *Daily Sentinel*. Marlon seemed to be particularly fawning around him.

"Everything all right, sir? Would you like another coffee? Some breakfast perhaps?"

Before the man could answer, Chester chipped in:

"I wouldn't eat here, pal. Food tastes like shit." Both he and Tyler collapsed into cackling laughter. Marlon glared at them, then turned back to the young man.

"Ignore them, sir. They're out on day release." He chuckled at his own joke but the young man's attention had been drawn to the figure of a young woman in a yellow tracksuit jogging towards them. He looked expectantly at Marlon, who nodded his head, then went back inside the café. His cowardly instincts dictated that he didn't want to be around when the shit hit the fan.

As Janine drew nearer, face flushed but beaming a brilliant wide smile, Tyler called out:

"Hey, young lady, how you doing? Come right over, we've got a chair all ready for…"

He broke off, noticing for the first time that there were only two chairs at the table, the ones on which he and Chester were seated. He stood up and went to fetch a spare chair from an adjoining empty table; just then, the young man got up and took a recording device from the inside pocket of his jacket. He walked towards Janine, holding the device out in front of him.

"Excuse me, miss. My name is Dan Challis, from the *Daily Sentinel*. Might I have a few words? I believe you are a humeleon. Would you grant me an interview? Tell the public what it's like to be a lizard?"

Upon hearing these words, Chester rose from his seat and took a swing at the reporter, knocking the recording device to the ground. Tyler took the few steps necessary to crush it underfoot.

"Fuck right off, mister," Chester said. "The lady ain't for talking."

Challis had recovered from the temporary shock of having the device knocked from his grip and looked defiantly at both of the old men. He said:

"Lady, you call that freak *a lady?*"

No further provocation was necessary. Despite his seventy-four years, Tyler swung at the reporter and landed a decently meaty blow on his jaw. Challis staggered backwards and fell on to the table at which he'd been seated, and both it and he collapsed to the ground. For good measure, Chester took a squeezy ketchup bottle and squirted the contents into the young man's face; the gooey red semi-liquid mixed with the blood on Challis' face, making it look as if he'd been struck several times by a professional boxer rather than by a septuagenarian author of books about bugs.

Marlon had come to the entrance to the café on hearing the commotion. Tyler looked at him and said:

"If I find out this is down to you, you'll get the same."

The café owner beat a hasty retreat back inside.

Chester took Challis' copy of the *Sentinel*, screwed it up, and threw it into the waste bin.

"Where that shit belongs," he said. "Although I can think of a better use for it, but I don't need to take a dump just yet."

Janine, who had been watching the proceedings with a mixture of shock and disbelief, walked up to Tyler and hugged him tightly. Tyler reddened deeply.

"Thank you, Mr Tyler," she said. "How the hell did that guy find out about me? About what I was?"

Chester looked at the sign above the café.

"I think Tyler is right. Look no further than Mr Marlon, who I always thought was a decent guy. Just proves how wrong you can be about people. How *he* found out, God knows; though I do seem to remember he was hovering around last Saturday when you...

51

your tracksuit… maybe he saw…"

Janine looked at the ground.

"So you guys knew, too?"

Chester reached out and tenderly lifted Janine's chin.

"We knew, but not until last weekend. Tyler noticed your arm. But I tell you what, young lady, it makes not a shit's worth of difference to either of us."

Janine smiled broadly and included Chester in her next big hug.

Chester noticed the grazing and small amount of blood on the knuckles of Tyler's right hand.

"Hey, come on, champ. Let's go back to my flat and get that cleaned up. That was some punch. Remind me never to piss you off."

Tyler and Janine burst into laughter. Chester continued:

"I feel like getting seriously drunk. Janine, you are cordially invited."

The three of them began to walk down the street. From somewhere came the steadily increasing wail of an ambulance, getting closer. Challis, who had by now managed to stand up somewhat shakily and was rubbing his numb face, hoped it was for him.

Chester unlocked the door to his ground-floor flat and the three friends walked into the bright and cheery interior. Chester motioned Janine and Tyler to his big, comfy-looking sofa and said:

"OK, what's it to be? I've got a bottle of Ireland's best whiskey for us, Tyler. White or red wine, Janine? Or you can have the same as us if you'd prefer. Or tea or coffee, of course. Don't want to tempt you into bad habits."

"Won't take much tempting, Mr Chester. White wine would be great."

"Cool. Just one thing, Janine; drop the 'Mr' you place so eloquently and politely in front of our surnames. We're plain old Tyler and Chester, we don't use first names! Tyler, I'll fetch the first aid kit as well."

Janine smiled. Chester walked through to his kitchen. Tyler said:

"You OK, Janine? Hopefully that nasty little scene didn't shake you up too much. Some people… I'm often ashamed to be human.

52

That reporter was straight out of the gutter. And Marlon. We'll never frequent that crap-hole again. Pardon my language, miss."

"Consider yourself pardoned... *Tyler*! And no, I'm fine. Geoff and I have put up with far worse, believe me. Thank you for coming to my rescue, I really appreciate what you did." She lapsed into a sudden silence, looking down at her lap. Tyler could tell something was troubling her.

"Tell me, Janine. What's bothering you?"

Janine looked hesitant. Just then Chester returned with their drinks on a tray along with a green plastic box with a red cross on the front.

"Janine?" Tyler persisted.

Chester sat down on the sofa on the other side of the young girl, a concerned look on his face matching Tyler's.

"Well, it's just that... the town where Geoff and I lived before we came here... well, we were driven out, we didn't leave by choice. Somehow our neighbours found out we were humeleons, although we'd been so careful..."

Janine was on the verge of tears. She recovered herself, then continued:

"It was horrible. Our house was burned down one night. Luckily we were still up and managed to escape before we were overcome by the flames. We left with nothing. And there were people... our neighbours, who we thought were friends, amongst them, jeering at us outside..."

The tears came once more and she gave way to them. Tyler took one of her hands gently in his; Chester took the other. Both men took generous gulps of their whiskey. Tyler offered Janine his glass.

"Take a sip, Janine. It will steady your nerves."

Janine did as she was bade; the fiery liquid made her splutter slightly but she took a second sip.

"Thank you, Tyler. That feels better. I'm scared that we'll be run out of this town now, just as we were beginning to settle down."

"That won't happen, Janine. By God, that will not happen. I know the editor of that tabloid paper, and I know where he spends his Friday and Saturday nights, and it's not with his wife. So I think we can count on him not to take the matter further. He'll tell that reporter to keep quiet, too, if he wants to keep his job. As for Marlon – he's just a coward and a chicken – the odd threat of physical violence will keep him quiet."

A silence descended between them. Then Chester said:

"Tell us about yourself, Janine. We feel that you have become a real friend to us, and God knows you don't get many new ones when you get to our age. But only if you want to; sorry, I'm not prying."

Janine smiled and wiped her eyes.

"That's OK, Chester." She settled herself more comfortably on the sofa and began:

"Geoff and I are twins. Our mother, we were later told, was a sex worker who'd volunteered for the experiment program, and having given birth to us, took her money and ran. Apparently she couldn't get out of that lab fast enough. We have no idea who our father was; one of our mother's many customers, we assumed.

"My earliest memory is of men and women in white coats monitoring and recoding everything we said and did. I'm sure you know what went on in that place. Some of the kids were born with more chameleon-like characteristics than human ones; I remember one boy we played with had protuberant eyes and a long tongue and struggled to see as we did or to communicate verbally. Others were stillborn and their bodies were quickly disposed of, we learned later. Incinerated. Geoff and I were lucky, I guess; our metabolisms had absorbed less of the chameleon DNA that we were injected with and so we looked and behaved more like humans. The dosage of chameleon DNA varied from foetus to foetus; I don't know why, because to this day I don't understand what the experiments were about or why they were carried out. It was only much later that we learned who and what we were without understanding the logic behind the experiments.

"We were treated well and we had plenty of food to eat and toys to play with. Later we were taught to read and write. We were happy and comfortable: this was our reality. Of course we didn't know any different. The staff were very kind to us. I remember escorted walks in a large garden at the back of the lab where there were donkeys. We were allowed to feed them carrots.

"Then one day – we would have been about six years old – we were told that we'd be going on a long journey at the end of the week to where some other people would be waiting for us and would look after us. We were too young of course, to know what was going on and cried when we had to leave. But the people – our foster parents – were a lovely professional couple in their early forties who couldn't have children of their own. They knew what we were, of course – humeleons – but they didn't mind and we were treated like any human kids would have been. In fact, we were doted on.

"Looking back, we did find it strange that we weren't allowed to mix much with other kids, and we were educated at home. Another memory is of watching my new mum take a shower; I didn't understand why she didn't have patches of scaly green skin on her arms, legs and back like Geoff and I had, which would often change colour dependent on the physical environment or what mood we were in; or a stump at the base of her spine where her tail would have been. Our tails were removed in the lab when we were just a few days old. Mum smiled and said we had those things because we were special, and best not to tell anyone else, or they'd get jealous and want those things, too. We were also given food just like we had at the lab, made up predominantly of mashed-up insects. Mum and Dad didn't eat that, so again Geoff and I thought we were special.

"We were in our early teens when our adoptive parents told us more about who and what we were and what had gone on in the lab and the circumstances of our birth. We learned that there had been a massive scandal and the lab had been forced to close, hence the need to have us adopted. Some kids weren't so lucky; those for whom parents couldn't be found were put down as humanely as possible. Because of our predominantly human attributes we were adopted quickly. We left our adoptive parents when we were eighteen.

"Geoff and I have found life difficult, as you can imagine. A real struggle. We are unable to form relationships and have lived together all our lives so far. Geoff runs his own business as an IT consultant and supports both of us. Sorry I've skipped over a fair few details but that, in a nutshell, is our history."

There was a long silence when Janine had finished her narrative. Both Tyler and Chester smiled indulgently at her and squeezed her hands tighter. Then Tyler spoke:

"Thank you for sharing all that with us, Janine. It must have been very difficult for you. It was dreadful what went on in that lab. Those experiments, the way it was all hushed up… if only I'd found out earlier… all my research…"

Both Chester and Janine turned puzzled, enquiring glances towards Tyler; but the old man seemed lost in a fog of vague remembrance and didn't elucidate further. Chester rose again and moved towards the kitchen. "I think we could all use another drink," he said.

Whilst he was out, Tyler rose from the sofa and moved towards one of Chester's bookshelves. He selected a volume at random – a history of Pre-Raphaelite art – and flipped through the pages. A photograph fell to the floor; Tyler bent down to pick it up. He was shocked at what he saw; his heart began to thud against his chest, his pulse was racing. The picture showed Chester aged somewhere in his early forties, smiling and shaking hands with Professor Julian Crown, the man in charge of operations at Larksoken Laboratories, the lab that had carried out the humeleon experiments. Tyler turned when he heard Chester re-enter the room. He held out the photo to his friend.

"Chester…?"

Chester didn't reply at first; merely put down the replenished drinks on the table and sat back down on the sofa. He had turned very white, and sat forward with his head bowed and his hands clasped together. Janine looked bewildered.

"Guys, what's going on? Tyler? Chester? Speak to me, I'm getting worried."

At last Chester looked up. "Sit down, Tyler, my old friend," he said gently. "You may need that drink when I've told you what I have to – need to – say. And another one straight after that. I would have told you this regardless of whether you had found that photo or not, in view of what Janine has said and what happened today."

Tyler sat back down. Chester, after some deliberation, as if he were juggling various thoughts in his mind, hesitantly continued:

"I'm not… I'm in no way proud of what I did or of my role in that whole goddamn business. It's true I was a biology teacher in those days, but I was also a consultant geneticist on the Humeleon Project. Wheels within wheels; I was at university with Julian Crown and he called me one day years later to offer me a position and money beyond my – beyond anyone's – wildest dreams. The trouble with academics very often is that they believe everything will remain theoretical. When I learned what was actually – physically – going on in that place, I secretly blew the whistle and brought it all down."

"You were Mr X?" Tyler asked.

"Yes. And I'm glad that I did what I did. I only got involved out of old-fashioned greed and the need for recognition in my field, for prestige. You know the rest. There was a huge scandal; the lab was closed, the experiments were brought to an end and the government toppled."

He took a sip of whiskey, then looked directly at Janine:

"Janine, I am so deeply, truly sorry for what we did and especially for my part in it. I've lived with the guilt for thirty years. I don't expect you to forgive me. What we did was inhuman – terrible – I can't think of enough words to describe it."

He lapsed into silence. Janine leant over and kissed him on the cheek.

"Chester, you have no need to apologize. What happened was terrible in many ways. But Geoff and I are happy and proud of who and what we are. Others weren't so lucky. But it wasn't all down to you. I can understand your need to keep quiet about it."

Chester smiled his thanks, a tear beginning to roll down his cheek. It was Tyler who spoke next.

"Just shows you never really know people huh, Chester? Janine – as it's now confession time there's something that I too need to get off my chest."

Janine and Chester turned towards him. Tyler looked directly at Janine.

"I nearly blurted it out earlier. Whilst I was in Madagascar, I wasn't just studying bugs. I did vast research into chameleons. What happened at Larksoken Laboratories was in part down to that research. I, too, apologize to you, Janine, and to Geoff, and for everything that went on in that vile institution."

Chester looked shocked.

"But Tyler… I never knew… this is crazy… we both worked on that project without knowing each other…"

"We were consultants, Chester, not lab workers. I never actually visited Larksoken or had any knowledge of who else was working on the Humeleon Project. It was classified, priority A1."

"Yes, of course," Chester said. I only went to Larksoken the once. Most of my business was conducted in secret meetings at Whitehall."

It was Tyler's turn for a huge kiss from Janine.

"Guys, what's done is done. We can't turn back the clock and remake the past. I'm glad it's all in the open though and you two can carry on being friends. So you didn't know about each other's involvement – that's understandable given what the business was all about and the secret nature of it."

Tyler got up and hugged Chester. The two men remain locked for several minutes. As Tyler sat back down again, he turned to Janine and said:

"Well, lovely lady, I hope that confessing all this makes us both… almost human."

BONESTAFF

Bonestaff leaned heavily on the spade he'd been using to dig up the last of the season's potatoes and grumbled at the pain his exertions had caused in what seemed like every bone of his septuagenarian body. Scanning the horizon, he noticed a heavy cloud of dust rise from the ground towards the sky of what was a cold but otherwise fine early autumn morning. Riders, he thought. A half-dozen of them, heading here, towards the abbey. The king's soldiers, no doubt, a party hunting for Deniers. There had been so many such hunting parties lately but none had stopped by here, perhaps taking for granted the Order's loyalty to the new monarch. Well, they'll find no Deniers here, Bonestaff thought; but if any happened to flee to the abbey they would find refuge and safe sanctuary here, without a doubt. The Order was firmly on the side of those who denied the ascension to the throne of the corrupt and evil Avric who had bloodily murdered his elder brother, the incumbent king, in an orgy of violence that had spread like wildfire across the land as Avric's followers seized every office of power and set about establishing the rule of tyranny, fear and suspicion.

As the riders neared the abbey Bonestaff saw that he had been wrong; there were five of them, not six. It was clear to him that one of their party must have perished; six was their usual number. Just a hundred yards away from where Bonestaff stood the riders halted, and the one of their number who was clearly in charge dismounted and walked towards the priest.

"Welcome, brothers, welcome to our abbey. Are you in need of refreshment after your... endeavours?" Bonestaff asked the advancing sergeant.

"No time, old man," the sergeant replied. He was now standing just three feet away from Bonestaff: a tall, imposing, threatening presence. But Bonestaff held his ground. He would offer hospitality to these soldiers but would not shrink away from them in fear or a show of obeisance.

"We have too many Deniers to hunt down and kill. There have

been reports of several in this area. Do you know anything of their whereabouts, priest? Perhaps you have some hiding away here, eh? Skulking around inside that ancient ruin of yours," the sergeant continued.

"There are no Deniers here, I assure you. Perhaps you would like to check for yourself? And the offer of refreshment still stands."

The sergeant hesitated, glanced back at his men, who looked tired, hot and thirsty.

"Well, if you have bread and wine to spare, priest, perhaps we could partake before we resume our hunt. We've been riding since the early hours and have had no break."

"Please, then, if you will all follow me?"

Bonestaff addressed this last remark to include the four other riders as well as the sergeant.

"By the way, I notice that there is one short in your party."

Bonestaff spoke to the sergeant as the two walked side-by-side towards the eastern cloister of the abbey, the other soldiers a short distance behind, chattering eagerly and laughing, relieved at the chance to have a rest, to eat and drink.

"A lucky shot from a Denier with a bow and arrow barely an hour ago. The arrow took my corporal straight in the eye and through the other side of his skull," the sergeant responded.

"Sounds like the work of a skilled archer, not the 'lucky shot' of an amateur." Bonestaff was smiling mischievously, an expression he hoped the sergeant couldn't see.

"A mere boy of fourteen. I put him to the sword. Made him swear loyalty to Avric before I slit his throat and gouged out his eyes and tongue. The crows we threw them to were very grateful for their free meal." The sergeant laughed heartily at his own humour. Bonestaff's expression had changed to one of shock, quickly followed by disgust. He shook his head in disbelief.

The abbey's refectory was down a short, dimly-lit corridor just off the eastern cloister. The air here smelled heavily of candlewax and dust. Bonestaff led the way through a large oak door and indicated the bench nearest to where the sergeant and his men had gathered, looking upwards at the high vaulted ceiling and the many stained glass windows which admitted long shafts of watery light.

"Please, gentlemen, be seated," Bonestaff implored them all.

The sergeant and his men scraped back chairs from the bench and sat down.

"I will seek out Brother Challis. Not a remarkable cook but I'm sure he will be able to prepare you something tasty and nutritious. I'll have wine and ale sent through, too."

The soldiers grunted their approval and Bonestaff left the refectory through a door opposite the one through which they'd all entered. On reaching the corridor outside he almost collided with Novice Yewing, who was rapidly approaching with a look of eager enquiry on his face.

"Ah, Abbott Bonestaff, sir... I hear we have visitors. But not the sort we should like to be overly welcoming to. Where are they, through there?" Yewing said, nodding towards the refectory.

"Yes, and we must be as welcoming as possible, albeit through gritted teeth, as it were. They may be soldiers of the Tyrant King but they are our guests, nevertheless," Bonestaff snapped.

Duly chastised, Yewing looked down at his feet. At just sixteen, he was the youngest of the Order, and the one most likely to unwittingly splutter out their opposition to the new monarch with his careless talk and silly chatter. He has a lot of maturing to do, Bonestaff thought. He also has a volatile and unpredictable temperament. Best to keep him out of the way.

"Now where is Brother Challis?" Bonestaff enquired of the young man. "I must get him to prepare food for our guests."

"In the kitchen garden," Yewing replied sulkily. "Gathering herbs."

"Good. Well get along to the library, Yewing. There are some new books that need classifying and putting away."

"But Brother Challis said I could help out in the kitchens... I'm learning to..."

"The library – now, Novice Yewing."

"Yes, Abbott."

Yewing shuffled away reluctantly in the direction of the library and Bonestaff walked as quickly as he was able towards the kitchen garden. Yewing, however, had no intention of going where he'd been ordered. Opening a door to his immediate right, he slipped through it and came out onto the west cloister. Walking briskly back in the direction of the kitchen, he slowed down as he reached the small garden where Brother Challis was plucking herbs from the ground whilst Abbott Bonestaff was talking to him about what food they should offer the soldiers. Yewing concealed himself behind a stone pillar.

"Well, there's the remains of last night's mutton stew," Challis said, raising himself from his crouching position and straightening his back.

"Oh, these creaking old bones… I could put a few extra items into that to spice it up a bit… make it a bit fresher tasting…"

"Do that, Brother Challis," Bonestaff said. Both men moved back into the kitchen. Yewing slipped out from his place of concealment, hopped unseen over the low garden wall, and ran into the nearby woods. If we're going to feed the Tyrant King's soldiers, he thought, I'll give them something they'll never have tasted before…

Yewing spent a lot of time in these woods and knew exactly where he was going and what he was looking for. Upon reaching a small clearing, he stooped down at the base of an oak tree and plucked six large, white conical fungi from the ground and stuffed them into the pocket of his habit. Retracing his steps back to the kitchen garden wall, he hopped back over and through the door into the kitchen, where Brother Challis stood alone, stirring the vast pot on the stove that contained the stew that was to be served to the soldiers.

"Ah, Yewing… where have you been, boy? Never mind, you're here now… take over stirring this, will you? I need to go to the pantry for some more cloves of garlic."

"Certainly, Brother Challis," Yewing replied, taking hold of the large wooden spoon that Challis thrust towards him. Whilst the latter pottered away towards the pantry, Yewing slipped the fungus he'd collected into the stew pot and commenced a vigorous stirring.

In the refectory the soldiers were in an uproarious mood as the effects of the abbey's strong home-brewed wine and ale took effect. It had been served to them in copious quantities by Novice Marsden, a young initiate like Yewing, who had been designated as their waiter. This he did with great reluctance but did not wish to disobey his masters. He hated these bastards as much as anyone in the Order. He had been especially shocked and horrified by the sergeant's retelling of the slaughter of the young fourteen-year-old boy in the nearby village earlier that day, a recounting that was now embellished with gorier details. When the sergeant had finished, his men laughed heartily and called for more drink. Something in the brief description the sergeant had given of the boy sent a flicker of recognition through Marsden's mind... corn-gold hair, blue eyes that stared up into the sergeant's own, pleading for mercy that wasn't shown... the small purple birth mark on his left cheek...

Bonestaff entered the refectory and, gaining Marsden's attention, indicated that the Novice should go to the kitchen. Evidently the meal was now ready to be served. Marsden made his way obediently to the kitchen from where he'd been standing at a respectful distance from the soldiers, moving only to refill their goblets and tankards. On reaching the kitchen, Marsden muttered a few words to Yewing.

"Novice Marsden, there is no time for idle chatter," Brother Challis barked. "The stew is now ready. Please take it to the refectory and serve it in the bowls from the cupboard there. Then return for the bread, cheese and ham."

"Yes, Brother Challis," Marsden replied. "Should I give them the cutlery to use from the cupboard also?"

"That would make perfect sense, don't you think?"

Yes, perfect sense, Marsden thought. *And perhaps I could stab the bastards with it.*

Marsden took the pot from the stove and moved to exit the kitchen. He paused only briefly to regard Yewing, who was standing by the doorway in an uncharacteristic silence.

"What's the matter, Yewing? Cat got your tongue? Please assist Marsden in the serving," Challis ordered the youth.

"For what they are about to receive, may the Lord make them truly thankful..." Yewing muttered solemnly, paraphrasing the pre-

63

meal prayer.

"What's that?"

"Nothing, sir. Let's go, Marsden."

Marsden placed cutlery and bowls before each soldier, into which Yewing began to serve generous helpings of hot, steaming stew. *Enjoy, you bastards,* Yewing thought. *It will be the last food you ever taste.*

"And keep the ale flowing!" the sergeant bellowed, as he and his men began eating noisily and greedily. *Like pigs at a trough,* Yewing thought.

"What are these mushrooms? They give this stew an interesting flavour." This from Aaron, who had assumed the mantle of corporal since the killing that morning.

"They're Latin name is *Amanita Virosa*," Yewing replied, "but they're more commonly known as 'Destroying Angel'."

"That's a curious name, how did they come to be known…"

But Aaron never got to finish his enquiry. All at once the soldiers began retching violently, clutching their stomachs and heaving. The sergeant and Aaron collapsed to the floor, struggling for breath. It was a pointless struggle… the other soldiers, also struggling for breath, choked and spluttered and finally they, too, collapsed. All of the soldiers' faces were contorted horrifically, their colour turning from deep scarlet to purple as they lost their fight for breath and expired with a few last choking and gurgling noises.

Yewing and Marsden, standing impassively by, offered no assistance; merely watched the horrible deaths of the soldiers with a grim fascination.

"What else did you put in that stew?" This from Marsden to his young co-Novice.

"A liberal helping of yew berries, just to make absolutely sure. Yew berries from Yewing!"

Both smiled at this, smiles which soon erupted into laughter.

Bonestaff gathered the other Brothers of the Order into the library a little later. Brothers Catchpole, Elias, Avery and Connick had been at work in or around the abbey, cleaning out rooms or working in the fields.

"Brothers," Bonestaff began, "we have today been joined at the abbey by five soldiers, a hunting party of the Tyrant King. Much as we despise the current regime for its treatment of the people, these soldiers are our guests and will be afforded such hospitality as befits our Order. They are currently in the refectory partaking of food and drink. Novices Yewing and Marsden are attending them. I propose that we seniors form an official welcoming committee. Leave your personal feelings aside. With any luck these men will be gone by nightfall with a good report of us here and will not trouble us again for some time, if ever."

There were murmurs of assent from the Brothers.

"Good, I take it that you agree. Come, we'll make our way to the refectory."

Yewing and Marsden were drinking what wine was left from the bottles that had been served to the soldiers. Not used to drink, both youths were feeling giddy. On hearing the approach of many feet and several voices, they both stood up from the bench on which they'd been sitting and did their best to appear both respectful and respectable.

"Remember, Marsden. This is down to me," Yewing said. "No intervening on my behalf. I'll take whatever punishment is due, I don't care. Justice has been served here today."

Marsden didn't reply, merely nodded. Both youths looked up as the full Order entered the refectory.

"Now then, gentlemen, how are the refreshments? Hope Challis hasn't poisoned you!" This from Bonestaff who swept briskly into the room ahead of the other Brothers. He stopped abruptly as his eyes took in the scene before him. Five dead soldiers sprawled in poses of agony across the floor beneath the bench on which they'd been sitting. The other brothers pulled up sharply behind Bonestaff, with expressions of horror and disbelief as they regarded the dead men.

"What in the Lord's name... what has happened here,

Yewing? Marsden? What has happened to these men?" Bonestaff cried in a high, quivering voice full of emotion.

"They are dead, Abbott Bonestaff. These bastards are dead and I killed them. And I'm glad I did. No regrets."

There was a cold steeliness to Yewing's voice that none of those assembled had heard before. The firm, confident voice of a man, not a callow youth.

"But why..." Bonestaff began, shaking his head.

"Because," spluttered Marsden, "they murdered my best friend this morning. That lad they were boasting about who shot and killed their corporal with the arrow. But more importantly, he was..."

"My brother," Yewing finished, looking the assembled Order straight in the eyes, one by one.

"And," said Challis, moving forward in front of Bonestaff, "my godson. I noticed you put those mushrooms and yew berries into the stew, Yewing. I could have stopped you but I didn't. I couldn't."

"We'll have to call on the Crowner and report this, of course," Bonestaff said in a voice that was quiet and barely audible to the others of the Order. They had assembled in the library.

"There'll be repercussions... Yewing, you will be hanged, my poor boy... They may even shut down the abbey... But that hardly matters now. Perhaps we'll all be hanged as Deniers..."

"Perhaps not." This from Brother Catchpole. The others looked at him eagerly, desperate for some means of escape from their predicament.

"What do you mean, Brother Catchpole?" Bonestaff said.

"I'm sure I'm right in assuming that nobody knows they ever came here? They were on a random tour of the surrounding countryside, hunting Deniers. They could gone anywhere. I say we bury those bastards under the flagstones on the yard outside the pigsty."

There was a nodding of heads and a murmur of assenting voices from those assembled.

"Gentlemen, gentlemen. Need I remind you that we are a

66

religious Order on sacred premises," Bonestaff said. The voices suddenly became quiet.

"Nevertheless," he continued. "We need to ensure that our Order continues its work in opposing the Tyrant King. This is a place of refuge, after all."

"And so?" This from Brother Elias, leaning forward eagerly.

"Collect your spades, Brothers. We have grim work ahead of us this night."

BRIDESMAIDS

The dresses were the most beautiful things either girl had ever seen. Bolts of pure white sleeveless chiffon with modestly cut necklines, ruffled from just below the breast to the hips, then a smooth sweep ending just above the knee. Their faces were alight with laughing smiles as they twisted and turned and cavorted in dances without music, revelling in their luxurious splendour which even the few still faintly visible bloodstains failed to spoil. Mordeth, the old hag, had made a good job of cleaning them and the material swished and glowed brightly as the girls sashayed in the crepuscular gloom of Semirg's lair.

In a damp, dark recess of his cavernous home, and completely unseen by the girls, Semirg watched them dance, a lascivious grin spreading across his twisted mouth. He began to dribble lustfully. They had certainly blossomed into fine specimens of human female pulchritude, and his mind flashed back to – how long ago had it been? Fifteen years, surely by now – to when he kidnapped them both on the same night and brought them here. They had been barely a couple of years old then – twins – and the abductions had been easy; he had materialized in their room as they slept innocently and simply spirited them away. He considered them to be more demon than human now. An admirable evolution which made him feel proud; a pride that he'd felt regarding all of his abductees over the years. But one of these girls would serve a very special purpose soon… but which to choose?

The one called Nicola, with her shoulder length blonde hair and bright blue eyes, was stubborn and headstrong, and took up a lot of his power to control her. She reminded him of a wild horse that resolutely refused to be broken, even after all these years. The other – Jayne – also blonde but with a light brownish tint, was the opposite: placid, malleable, and therefore less demanding on his powers. Both would make suitable bridesmaids for Alice, his human bride-to-be, at their upcoming wedding ceremony, which would also mark her full transition from human to demon. He had bowed to Alice's wish for bridesmaids, but would allow her only one, and he would choose her. He was the one in control, after all... wouldn't do to show weakness toward these creatures, whom he still didn't fully trust, by acceding to every demand they made. No, it was to be one bridesmaid only, just to please her on that special day, and the chosen one would be kept alive as a surrogate wife should Alice fail to live up to his expectations. The other would be killed, sliced up and fed to his hounds. The thought made him begin to salivate all the more.

"Nicki, do you remember anything of our lives before we were brought here?"

It was half an hour later, and the girls had folded their dresses away and were now seated on the large bed they shared in what passed for a bedroom in that miserable place.

"Before we were abducted and enslaved, you mean?" Nicola replied, a flash of anger in her voice. "Brought here to do the bidding of our lord demon master and his vile extended family?"

Then, seeing the meek, forlorn look on her sister's face, she adopted a more conciliatory tone.

"No, very little, I'm afraid. Semirg has been very successful in wiping out large parts of our memories. And you?"

Jayne looked up from her lap, where her hands were clasped tightly together, and stared at the far, bare wall that constantly seeped small trickles of water. There was a far-away look in her eyes.

"I vaguely remember that doll we always fought over... Anna?" A small, sad smile came to her lips. "And a holiday once, sunny, light-filled days when we were incredibly happy. But I don't remember Mum and Dad much."

She looked back into her lap again. The smile had disappeared.

Nicola hugged her sister but said nothing. There was only a matter of a few minutes between them but a gulf in the level of emotional toughness. Throughout their years-long ordeal it was Nicola who had tried to stay strong for both of them, hoping – no, resolutely determined – that they would escape; that one day Semirg's hold over them would diminish sufficiently for them to be able to go back to the world from which they had been cruelly snatched. She lightly kissed the top of Jayne's head, and sighed deeply. Poor, dear, lovely Jayne. Nicola was surprised she had survived this long. She seemed resigned to the life Semirg had thrust upon them: was willing and subservient. But she didn't resent her sister for that, didn't regard her as weak. It was her coping mechanism, and made Nicola all the more determined to see them both through this, made her feel more protective towards the fragile, delicate girl she considered to be her 'little sister'.

Jayne suddenly looked up, a quizzical expression creasing her brow.

"Alice is very beautiful. And human, too, of course, like us. I wonder if she can remember much, if anything, of *her* past life?"

Nicola stood up and stretched; they didn't get much exercise and their dancing earlier had made her feel stiff and slightly weary.

"Who knows?" Nicola replied. "Perhaps we should ask her before she becomes a fully-fledged demon." She hadn't intended there to be any humour in this statement but they both collapsed into giggles.

"Such a pity if she turns into an old hag like Mordeth," Jayne said wistfully. "Perhaps, though, even she was beautiful once."

Thinking of Mordeth also brought thoughts of the brides-maid's dresses they had been wearing.

"If we ever get out of here I'm going to dance and dance and dance every day until I drop!" Jayne said. Nicola sat back down beside her sister once more.

"Yes, and in something better than those bloodied rags that Semirg stole from the bodies of more of his victims. Whoever they were, poor souls."

Jayne looked horrified. "But I thought you enjoyed dancing in them? You said your dress was the most beautiful thing you'd ever seen. You were delighted, enchanted..."

"I got carried away. We don't get much in the way of nice things here, do we? Perhaps I was thinking more of what they looked like when they were originally made. Of how those poor girls loved them and how they looked in them. I tried not to notice the blood stains. I was so happy to see *you* happy, darling sister."

"Yes, I know. And I haven't forgotten those poor girls either.

70

Perhaps they were just like us."

"Yes, perhaps. But they were free. Even in death, they were free."

Their thoughts and conversation were suddenly interrupted by the rolling, bellowing thunder of Semirg's voice, demanding their immediate attendance.

Alice sat alone in her chamber, contemplating her reflection in the cracked mirror and brushing her luxuriantly long, chestnut-coloured hair. She should be happy, she thought; as any bride-to-be should feel happy. Even though she was marrying a fat, bloated demon with ugly, leathery skin like that of a rhinoceros. But it had not been a matter of considering *whom* she was marrying, but rather looking forward to and enjoying the ceremony itself. She had sufficient of her old memories still intact to recall the one wedding she had attended as a little girl – she had been a bridesmaid, although she couldn't remember who the bride was – and how happy and full of joy she'd been. And determined that one day she, too, would be a beautiful bride with a pure white dress and be the centre of attention, everyone turning to look at her as she walked down the aisle, smiling broadly behind her veil. But doubts had begun to creep in during these last few days before the wedding, and she couldn't put her finger on what it was that was troubling her. She had put it down initially to the fact that all brides got nervous before the big day, and often had second thoughts. Now she wasn't sure that was the root cause. She was getting an increasing number of flashbacks to her old life, before she had been abducted and brought here by Semirg. She had been no older than Nicola and Jayne then, and that had been ten years ago. But the twins had been much younger when they had been brought here. Recent conversations with Jayne, though, had revealed that she, too, was not only remembering, but yearning for her previous life. Semirg's power had been very strong and his mental grip on them absolute up to now, but, given the fact that she was starting to recall more, as was Jayne, she was beginning to feel that that power was waning. Perhaps she could do better for herself than this sham ceremony? Did she really want to

71

become a demon, after all? She was feeling a stronger impulse in the opposite direction; the need to become more human, not less. Semirg was sitting cross-legged on the floor of his lair in a circle with several friends and members of his family. It was the evening before his wedding day and he was feeling rather smug and self-important at the thought of his imminent nuptials. They were engaged in the business of having several rounds of celebratory drinks and the mood was getting increasingly rowdy. Semirg felt, however, that some entertainment was necessary, and called Mordeth the hag over to him, and the aged crone leant down to hear her master's command. After a few seconds she shook her head in understanding and left the gathering, heading to Nicola and Jayne's room. Half an hour later, the twins appeared, dressed in their bridesmaids' dresses, and Semirg bade them dance for the gathering. The twins, who had already been baffled by the order to don their wedding attire and attend the party, wondering what could possibly be in store for them, now looked around themselves nervously, unsure of what exactly to do. Whereas dancing in private (as they hadn't noticed Semirg's presence at the time, and so had believed themselves to be alone and unobserved) had been as natural as breathing, and had brought them rapturous joy, this performance was awkward, humiliating and totally devoid of any co-ordination or free-flowing movement. Semirg was disappointed, he had hoped for a repeat of what he had seen a few days previously. But the guests didn't seem to mind. They regarded the human female performers with a mixture of jealousy and desire, and one in particular – Danok, Semirg's young nephew – was completely and utterly besotted. In truth it was not the first time he had seen the twins, but never dressed like this, in those dresses... and he had, for many a month, longed for and desired Alice, his uncle's intended bride. He decided to act, knowing that what belonged to one demon could quickly be acquired by another, family or not. He could hardly contain his lust and excitement, and when the girls had finished their shambolic performance and returned to their room, he waited for a short while then rose, begging Semirg's pardon for his early departure, but citing that he had pressing business that night, and would see his uncle at the following day's ceremony. His departure was hardly noticed as the party got into full, uproarious swing.

Danok hurried down the main passage of the lair and went in search of the girls in the multitude of rooms that led off from it.

"I can remember a book that mum used to read to us before we went to sleep," Jayne said. "It was about the adventures of a bear, and a young boy was in it… Christopher something. I can see Mum leaning over us as she read, checking to see if we were still awake or not. I think she enjoyed the stories as much as we did. I still can't make out Mum's face, though, but I can definitely feel the deep sense of love she had for us."

She was sitting on the bed with Nicola beside her once more, and Alice sat cross-legged in front of them, her face beaming with a wide smile, enraptured by Jayne's words. It was not long after the girls had had to perform their humiliating dance and they still wore their bridesmaid's dresses. Then Nicola said:

"Yes, I'm beginning to remember those stories too. There was a donkey… Eeyore!"

Jayne laughed. "Yes! Eeyore! Oh, those stories were wonderful." Suddenly her eyes began to moisten with tears.

"Oh, Nicki, I miss Mum so much. And I think I'm starting to remember Dad. He was always buying us presents even when it wasn't our birthday or Christmas."

Nicola looked tenderly at her sister. Then Alice said:

"I'm beginning to remember stuff from my old life, too. I went to a school where I had violin lessons after normal lessons had finished. And I was really good at science and French. I had a friend called Jenny Peters and we both fancied Mr Harris, our Geography teacher."

The girls lapsed into silence, then Nicola said:

"I think Semirg's power over us is diminishing."

"Yes," Alice concurred, "I think you're right."

"Nicki, does that mean we can go home now?" Jayne said. "Please say we can. I want to find Mum and Dad again. And we must take Alice with us."

Nicola rubbed her sister's shoulder.

"We're going home, Jayne. Back to the life that is rightfully ours."

Jayne could barely contain her excitement. She hugged Nicola and then Alice in turn.

Danok was becoming increasingly frustrated as he ran through the myriad tunnels of the cave in search of the girls. Everywhere he turned seemed to lead to a dead end and several times he stopped, hoping to hear the sound of any conversation they may be having to use as a guide to their exact location. But he could hear nothing. Perhaps they had retired to bed. He carried on running down the main passage he was in and was about to reach another dead end when he saw candlelight glowing from the entrance of what looked to be a large chamber on his left. Surely this was it? He slowed down, not daring to believe that he could finally be at the girls' chamber and in imminent reach of his prize. Or prizes...

And now he could distinctly hear voices; female human voices, his acute hearing picking up their hurried conversation and laughter. He rushed towards the light and into the chamber; the girls, alarmed at the demon's sudden presence, began to scream.

"Hush, hush, keep quiet, you little bitches," Danok commanded. "You'll have my fat useless uncle and his friends down upon us in no time. I mean you no harm. That's better... now, how would you feel about getting away from here, eh? How does that sound?"

Jayne looked quickly at Nicola, and then at Alice. Nicola said defiantly:

"And what would be expected of us in return? Would we not be going from one hopeless situation to another? At least here we know what is likely to happen to us, how things will work out. We have no way of being able to trust you, demon."

Danok began to laugh. "You have no idea, have you? My uncle intends to marry you – the one called Alice – and keep one other as a surrogate wife. Their ultimate fate is far from certain should Alice live up to his expectations. You younger ones will both play the part of bridesmaids at the wedding ceremony and then the one not selected as the alternative bride will be killed. Come with me

74

and I guarantee that all three of you will live."

The girls looked confusedly at one another, unsure what to do, uncertain whether Danok spoke the truth. Trusting any demon was surely a foolhardy thing to do. But all three knew one thing: that Semirg's power over them was waning, and therefore they had a faint glimmer of a chance to escape. To go with Danok would surely mean becoming totally enslaved once more. Better the devil you knew…

Semirg became suddenly alarmed, and lowered the goblet from his mouth before taking another sip. Something was wrong: very, very wrong. Although he had recently acknowledged to himself that his powers over the girls were beginning to diminish, he still had sufficient of it left to realise that somehow he was in danger of losing control over Alice, Nicola and Jayne. And then another image came into his mind: his nephew, Danok. So that is why Danok left the celebration early, he thought. That was the 'business' that he had to attend to that night – stealing the girls away from him. He dropped the goblet to the ground, stood up, and began to move swiftly to Jayne and Nicola's chamber, where he sensed that the current drama was taking place.

"Where are you going, Semirg?" one of the revellers shouted after him. "Not bailing out of the celebration early, I hope?"

Semirg ignored him, and began to run.

"Come on, come with me!" Danok implored. "I will treat you well enough, as much as humans deserve to be treated, that is."

Still the girls hesitated. They were seated next to each other on Nicola's bed, arms around each other, trembling with fear and uncertainty.

Danok suddenly became aware of a presence behind him. He turned slowly.

"So, treacherous nephew, you would steal my girls away from me? Why would you do this? Have I not shown you all the kindness and courtesy that family and the demon brotherhood demands? Speak! I will hear your testimony before meting out punishment."

Danok didn't reply; he looked around as surreptitiously as possible for a weapon with which to attack Semirg and overpower him. His eyes alighted on an inverted cross made of brass in a corner of the room. With a swift movement he ran towards it and grabbed it, and then, turning, hurled it with all the youthful strength he had at his uncle. Semirg had no chance to react. The cross spun towards him and smashed into his skull, sending him staggering backwards with a cry of pain. He fell. This gave Danok all the opportunity he needed: he sprang upon the prostrate body and plunged his dagger into Semirg's heart. Semirg gurgled hideously and expired within seconds. Danok rose and turned towards the girls.

"Now see what your hesitation has made me do! If you'd come with me as soon as I demanded my uncle would still have lived! Come quickly, the other demons will sense something is wrong and be here soon."

Jayne had begun to sob uncontrollably, her face turned into her sister's breast. Alice looked on, shocked, unable to speak.

Danok moved towards them but stopped, suddenly, his face contorted with pain; he staggered forwards and then fell. There was a large silver dagger protruding from between his shoulder blades.

Behind him, in the entrance to the chamber, another demon stood. Several seconds of silence fell before he spoke.

"Go, humans. Get out of here. There is no reason for you to be here anymore."

Alice stood, hesitantly, and held out her hand to Nicola and Jayne; they too stood, and all three walked towards the entrance of the chamber, walking past the demon who had slain Danok. The demon stood aside to let them pass.

Alice knew the way out of the caves, and after walking and stumbling for several minutes, the girls emerged into the fading light of an early autumn dusk. Alice strode purposely forward, whilst Nicola supported Jayne. After about half a mile, Nicola shouted:

"Alice, stop! We must rest. Jayne can't go on, she's too weak. Surely we are safe now."

Alice stopped, turned, and nodded her head. They sat beneath the branches of an ancient, gnarled oak tree. They were silent for many minutes, unable to take in what had happened but were relieved and glad to be free at last. It was Jayne who spoke first. She looked up into her sister's face.

"Maybe one day we'll be real bridesmaids, Nicki."

"Perhaps," Nicola replied. "Perhaps."

She leaned down and kissed Jayne lightly on the forehead.

Alice smiled, relieved that their ordeal was over.

DUMMIES

There were three of them, stood next to each other like shy strangers at a party. They struck ridiculously unnatural poses; intended by the manoeuvring of human hands of their solid wax bodies to look humanlike; but they failed, miserably.

All three were naked.

The dummy in the middle of the three, by dint of the two protuberant mounds on its chest, was obviously intended to be female. Despite the ridiculous charade of the attempt to make them appear human, the two either side of her could have been said to appear like potential suitors. Shy potential suitors at a party of strangers, both of them unwilling to break the ice, to make the first move.

Their expressions gave nothing away; all three had straight moulded waxen lips that neither smiled nor scowled. But there was something about their eyes; something that could be said to be vaguely human in the way they began to glimmer, to sparkle, and to come to life. They smiled with their eyes.

Eventually, as even the most reticent of strangers in an enclosed social environment are wont to do, one of them began to move its lips in an attempt to speak, but all that came was a low, guttural gurgle. It tried several more times, then gave up. For now.

Outside the long-abandoned shop, once a thriving evening costume for sale-or-hire business, with its cracked front window smeared with fly shit and street grime, the harsh winter wind began to howl, gathered speed, and the glass which had resisted such pummelling for so long finally shattered completely. The dummy that had attempted speech raised its left arm and pointed at the freshly-made hole in the glass, the shards sparkling like diamonds inside the premises, and the other two knew, with no need for verbal communication, exactly the meaning it attempted to convey. Stepping stiffly down from the podium on which they stood, all three moved towards the newly-formed exit. The furious wind bellowed, crashed heavily in rapid blasts against the rickety, aged door. It began to snow, but the dummies, for all their nakedness, felt no cold.

Colm McKenzie, much-loved but often to be avoided town drunk, staggered along the street from where he'd just exited the Plough Inn toward the general direction of his lowly bedsit. Two days to go until Christmas Day, and Colm was full of Yuletide spirit (and beer.) He carried his copy of the *Daily Mirror* (news unread, all puzzles duly filled in) rolled up in the pocket of his voluminous overcoat and hoped that perhaps he might get some nice, warm gloves from the church Christmas charity give-away that he would be attending in the morning (no – today; he quickly looked at his antique watch and realized it was Christmas Eve already). He tilted his head upward and regarded the vast firmament, noticed the stars scattered like sequins on black velvet. "Ah, even when you're pissed you have a poetic turn of mind, Mr McKenzie," he thought. As he once more turned his attention to more earthly sights, what he saw next was like a vision from his deepest erotic imaginings; a naked woman (OK, albeit totally bald) was walking stiffly, awkwardly towards him (his first thought was: "she looks as tight as me.") He did not, at first, notice the two equally stiffly-walking 'minders' following behind her at a distance of thirty yards. Buoyed up by the courage gained from his alcohol intake, Colm was determined to make the most of this Christmas gift from heaven.

"Hey, darling, you looking for a bed for the night?" he bellowed across the street. The woman seemed not to notice him; Colm wasn't deterred, as the unforgivingly cold wind had very likely ripped and twisted his words to inaudibility.

"You there, love, want some company to keep you warm? You must be freezing. Come over here and share my overcoat." Colm was nothing if not a complete gentleman.

The figure seemed to notice him for the first time and crossed the street towards him. Colm then noticed something through his alcohol-induced fuzziness; that despite appearing to be naked, the girl had no nipples on her breasts and no pubic hair. Colm thought crazily that perhaps she was on her way home from a Christmas fancy dress party where her costume had merely consisted of an all-over, flesh-coloured body suit. He unwound the tinsel from around his neck (stolen from the pub Christmas tree) and held it out towards the advancing girl, intending to place it around her neck. But he never got chance. Only a couple of feet from him, the girl raised her right arm and brought her balled fist crashing down on Colm's skull. The blow was heavy; Colm sank to his knees as blood began to pour from the wound it had caused. He was dead within seconds. The post-mortem would later reveal death by heart failure brought on by shock.

Across the street, the two attendant male dummies had found the power of further facial expression. As well as their bright, gleaming eyes, both now wore smiles of approval for what their companion had done. There was an insanely evil aspect to those smiles; an evil act was making them more human by the minute. The one who had attempted speech in the shop now tried again, and succeeded: *"Good!"* however, was all it managed to say, but it was enough. Both male dummies then blew her a kiss; this scenario was taking on all the aspects of a ritual courtship.

Brian Kellwood lifted his glass and took another swig of ice-cold lager. Spread out in front of him on the pub table were several printouts from various internet searches he'd done that morning concerning local crimes through the ages; these he intended to use as research material for the book he planned to write.

It was early doors, just a week to go until Christmas, and Brian intended having a few drinks in an attempt to enter the Yuletide spirit before the descending hordes of party animals took over the establishment. He hated crowds, especially Christmas crowds with their boringly inane conversations that rose to shouting levels as the drink flowed more freely and the music got louder.

Most of the material he'd printed out failed to spark his imagination; a disappointing haul for the book he was intending to write; all except one story, an incident that occurred just three years ago. Brian remembered the incident well, had covered it in fact when he was a mere junior reporter on the local newspaper but had forgotten about it. It was the report of a man who claimed that his drinking pal had been assailed and murdered "by shop window dummies." Brian smiled at the memory; he had himself interviewed this man, an unfortunate, shambling alcoholic just as the murdered man had been.

That the victim's pal had been murdered there was no doubt; the Coroner's verdict had been "murder by person or persons unknown." Subsequent police investigations had turned up nothing – there had been no forensic evidence to work with at all. No weapon was ever found. The pal – Gordon Travis – had fallen under suspicion himself at one point – a fall-out amongst drunks being the view taken – until it was pointed out by the pathologist that the positioning of the fatal blow meant that it could hardly have been administered by a man a good six inches shorter than the deceased. Travis had admitted that they'd "had words" in the pub, but stated that after a few minutes he'd decided to go after his friend – who'd left in a huff (having no more money for another drink. Travis had enough for two, hence the quarrel, but had decided that he would stand another round after all for the sake of the spirit of Christmas. He had been no more than a hundred yards from the retreating figure of McKenzie when he'd seen the assault take place, before the assailants – the "shop dummies" – had shuffled away in the opposite direction. Travis, in shock and disbelief, hid in a side-alley next to the pub, then re-entered the watering hole when he felt it was safe to do so in order to use the public telephone to call the police. The police had, of course, resolutely refused to lend even a grain of credence to the Travis' statement.

Brian – who still worked on the local newspaper – knew that the police still intermittently put out requests for fresh information – witnesses to come forward, etc., often through the paper itself. But nobody had as yet come forward, no fresh evidence had been gathered. Brian doubted there ever would be – who was bothered about a murdered drunk? His wistful smile turned into a sorrowful expression of regret and sadness. He knew his philosophy to be true as today's increasingly self-centred society and insular communities wouldn't even give this incident the time of day; if not then, certainly not now. Not even at Christmas. He gathered his papers together, shoved them haphazardly into the shoulder bag he'd brought with him, finished his beer, and left the pub; wondering as he went if Travis was still alive, and if so, whether he would be willing for another interview regarding the case.

But further research into the life of Travis proved virtually fruitless. After the death of his friend, Travis had become a born again non-drinker, made an attempt to clean up his act, and had become a community youth worker. Two years later he had been bequeathed a large sum of money by a well-to-do aunt (his only living relative) and had subsequently moved to Canada. Well, fair play, Kellwood thought, although he cursed the fact of having arrived at a dead end. What proved more fruitful, however, was his wider internet research the following morning into local unsolved murders outside the remit of his newspaper, which he undertook purely on a whim. He extended the search countywide and was amazed at the result: five in total since the death of McKenzie. He reached for his notebook and began to scribble furiously.

"Sorry to bother you, sir, but there's a gentleman down here asking to see you. Brian Kellwood, a local journalist. Says he may have new information appertaining to the dummy murder. You remember – the McKenzie case, sir?"

Inspector Bryant heaved a massive sigh and said: "OK, Sergeant, show him up" and replaced the telephone receiver onto its cradle. He had a dreadful feeling that this wasn't going to be a good day. He had been feeling particularly dyspeptic that morning ("must tell Anne to put a little less chilli in the con carne," he'd mentally noted to himself.) A couple of minutes later there was a knock at his door and Kellwood entered his office. Having taken a seat, but with no preamble whatsoever, Kellwood began speaking; Bryant noted instantly that he seemed the nervous, excited sort. Let him speak, Bryant thought. Just let him have his five minutes of glory then I'll show him the door. Politely, of course.

"I take it that your sergeant has explained why I'm here and the fresh evidence I may be able to offer to your investigation. The results of my research shows that there have been five unsolved murders in the last three years across the county. Six if you include McKenzie, the one in our own town. And why wouldn't you include him? It seems to be where it all started. These murders could well be connected: all victims were male, all were attacked within a ten-mile radius, and all were killed in the lead up to the Christmas period by heavy blows to the head. No murder weapon has ever been found and there is a total lack of human forensic material on the victim's bodies, ergo no DNA to work with. In two of the cases – McKenzie's included – there is witness testimony alluding to 'strange, naked figures' seen in the immediate vicinity of the crimes. 'Like shop dummies, they were. Human, but not human, if you understand what I mean. They walked funny, all stiff.' That was a direct quote from one such witness, Gordon Travis, who says he saw the McKenzie murder happen."

Bryant didn't reply at first, he merely regarded his visitor across the desk, weighing him up. Was this personal, or professional interest? Kellwood sat forward in his chair, looking at the Inspector like a child eager to be believed. As the latter remained impassive, Kellwood felt obliged to carry on. He was well used to the cynicism of the police which needed no verbal expression, just a non-committal silence.

"Well, Inspector? What do you think? Surely this means a fresh investigation is warranted? It's my belief that we could be dealing with the supernatural here. You'll remember no doubt the incidence of old man Sherwood's shop, the premises in Maple Street? It had lain empty for six months since his death, then it was reported that the shop window had been smashed to smithereens and that the three dummies positioned on a pedestal within the window, that had once been adorned with Sherwood's evening dress creations, were missing. It was presumed to be the work of vandals; however, what the public wasn't told – nor the local press at the time, shame on you – was that it was noticed by a particularly vigilant constable that *the glass had been broken from the inside. It was lying in thousands of fragments on the pavement outside."* This happened the same night as McKenzie's murder!"

Kellwood sat back in his (rather uncomfortable) chair with the air of one who had delivered a devastating blow of logic that would surely end the debate: a *fait accompli.* Bryant at last felt compelled to speak; but merely said, "Follow me, Mr Kellwood." At this, he rose from his own chair and walked out of the office. Kellwood too stood up and followed the Inspector dutifully down several corridors, up two flights of stairs, and out onto a fire escape. Kellwood was briefly seized by the mad idea that Bryant was going to throw him from these giddy heights to the ground below. But the policeman, continuing in enigmatic mode, said: "That 'vigilant constable' to whom you referred is now a detective sergeant." Kellwood was unsure how to respond as Bryant reached inside his jacket pocket and pulled out a crumpled pack of cigarettes, and offered one to Kellwood, who shook his head in refusal. "Gave up six months ago." Bryant uttered a dismissive grunt and lit his smoke, before speaking once more.

"Mr Kellwood, what you say is very interesting but you outline things that are already known to me. I was aware of the other murders – outside our Division of course but we *do* communicate with one another. But what I don't need are patterns; my wife knits, she's got hundreds of 'em. What I need are *hard facts*, not a load of superstitious nonsense, either. Supernatural, my arse. The two witnesses you describe are hardly reliable – one was a hopeless drunk who probably also saw Santa Claus that night: the other was a lonely, partially-sighted, rather eccentric elderly lady who may well spend her days imagining all kinds of things. This hardly engenders much confidence as to their testimony."

Kellwood was determined to pursue this as far as he could, however. Or at least as far as the barrier of the Inspector's stubborn cynicism would allow him before he became overwhelmed by the desire to shake the policeman roughly by the lapels of his jacket. Assaulting a police officer was hardly going to help his case...

"But, Inspector, you're missing the point. With no realistic possibility, or probability, of collusion they claim to have seen the *same thing* on the nights of those murders. Both claim to have seen shop dummies at or near the scene. Not physical, hard evidence, granted – but surely this strikes you as odd, to say the least?"

The Inspector grunted once more. "Travis claimed he saw dummies. The elderly lady – Mrs Sherrod, I believe her name was – probably saw or heard this on the local news and imagined she saw the same thing. As I said, she was, or is, rather eccentric. There goes your so-called evidence, Mr Kellwood. Now I don't mean to be rude or off-hand but I have an in-tray of outstanding work that nearly stretches up to the ceiling of my office. If you'll follow me down, I'll show you the way out. I will say, however, that if you *do* come across any hard evidence please get back in touch. We often put out fresh appeals for help from the public regarding cold cases, as I'm sure you're aware."

Kellwood stood motionless in stunned disbelief for a few seconds and then followed Bryant down the fire escape. He couldn't believe Bryant's pig-headed refusal to see things that were so obviously clear, and rejected the policeman's view on the connecting fact of the dummies. It was too dismissive, too easily explained away, too pat. It was almost as if he was attempting to hide something, some deeper knowledge of these crimes. Well, if what was required was hard evidence, he'd get it; this was now becoming a personal mission and Kellwood was starting to feel the zeal of the religious fanatic. It helped combat the uneasy feeling he had that Bryant saw him as a complete fool, and that he had been humiliated. What he wasn't to know was that this was the first and last time that he'd see Bryant alive.

Bryant returned to his office after showing Kellwood out of the building and looked despairingly at the growing mountain of paperwork on his desk. For such a small town, they seemed to have a disproportionately high crime rate. He glanced hopefully at the clock on the wall, and then grinned widely: almost six thirty, time to go home. He'd had more than enough for today, and his interview with Kellwood had left him feeling drained and uneasy. Sure, the man had a point. Several points in fact. The truth was that he had been deeply worried by the so-called 'dummy murders', they had plagued his dreams as well as his waking moments these last five years. He'd done all he could on limited resources to investigate the murders, and felt frustrated by the lack of progress both locally and across the county. Perhaps Kellwood was right – they *were* dealing with the supernatural here, hence the lack of hard physical evidence that he needed in order to solve them. He thought ruefully that perhaps they – the police – were the dummies. Sighing heavily, he decided that a pint or two before Emily's roast beef dinner was in order (his dyspepsia had thankfully subsided and he began to feel hungry once more, accentuated by the fact that he'd skipped lunch.) Yes, a couple of pints in the Plough were just what he needed right now, and Emily rarely dished-up dinner before nine.

The atmosphere in the Plough Inn was convivial to say the least. One of the establishment's best features (besides its fine selection of real ales) was a roaring log fire that, in addition to the alcohol, induced feelings of happiness and contentment that were helping to turn Bryant's mood around completely for the better. He felt comforted by the buzz of anonymous conversation that droned on all around him; the pub wasn't completely full as yet – no doubt the Christmas revellers would be arriving later. He thought of some lines of a poem by Robert Browning, remembered from his far-off schooldays: "God's in his heaven, all's right with the world." Well, if God was a pint of Old Speckled Hen and a gloriously warm fire, then Bryant was a true believer and no mistake. He chuckled at his own wit.

He was at the bar ordering his third pint when he glanced at the clock behind the counter: eight-fifteen. He would have time to drink this nectar and be back in plenty of time for his dinner. Life certainly wasn't so bad after all. He put his earlier grim mood down to the fact that it was Monday; surely the most depressing day of the week. Yet he couldn't completely take his mind off his earlier conversation with Kellwood; various details swirled continually around his poor brain. Dummies… murder… the supernatural… unsolved crimes… his continual gripes about lack of resources in order to investigate things thoroughly, which he'd hinted at to Kellwood. The lack of real co-operation from the other forces across the county. They were a backwater, what did they matter, despite his growing case-load? Well bugger it, he could only do what he could do. This third pint was tasting better than the previous two and it didn't seem to matter anymore. His thoughts turned instead to roast beef, roast potatoes, garden peas, thick gravy... and perhaps his favourite rice pudding to follow. Quick brandy and then the glorious oblivion of his bed.

The night was black-ink dark and a heavy, muffled atmosphere promised substantial snowfall. The silence was such that a robin's sweet fluting song that rose from a tree opposite the Plough Inn could surely have been heard for miles around. It spoke of regret for the passing of summer and hopes for the coming spring. It could certainly not have prophesied violent death; such is the innocence of nature in comparison to man's potentially violent fate.

In the alleyway at the side of the pub the dummies stirred once more, determined, as they awoke, to resume their awkward, rigid, macabre courtship ballet of death. The female dummy was the first to consciousness from their period of stasis and was feeling hungry for male attention; the two male suitors, now coming to consciousness themselves, were determined to pursue what they felt instinctively was their natural rite. Time meant nothing to them, this dance could last forever. What mattered was wooing the lady, even to the extent of committing murder themselves. So far she had done all the killing to draw them and stoke their desires; she was a *femme fatale*. Surely now it was time for them to reciprocate with a killing of their own, to show their devotion, to demonstrate their increasing assimilation of human feelings and emotions. Did they feel any sort of rivalry? Perhaps. But both males felt so certain that they would win their lady that they hardly cared about the other. Both were prepared to bide their time and go as far as eternity if that is what it would take to win her.

Bryant exited the Plough Inn (somewhat reluctantly) at ten minutes to nine. Not that he wasn't looking forward to his homely comforts; just that the new barrel of ale and the warmth of the pub's interior had instilled within him a contentment which, despite the relative smooth running of his home and married life, he very rarely felt in the wider context that included his professional life. He was thinking how long he would have to go until retirement; just two more years until he was free of the burden of his job and professional responsibility and could concentrate on his hobbies of gardening, painting and writing detective stories (he was determined to get published before he died. Just to leave something behind, one single short story, to be remembered by when his garden was overgrown and his weak, watery paintings had faded.) Such were his feelings that he didn't hear the awkward, clumsy footsteps lurching behind him; and certainly hardly felt the heavy, crushing blow on top of his skull, just a momentary sensation of pain. He fell to the ground in total bewilderment; what the hell was happening to him? He was aware of the sensation of pain but the alcohol was cushioning the shock. Just to make sure that the deed was done, the male dummy rained further blows down onto Bryant's head until the resultant gurgling finally stopped. Blood spread across the pavement like water seeping from an old, rusted bucket, and the inspector of police was finally dead. The dummy, now satisfied, looked across the street to his two companions and roared a primeval cry that brought a corresponding, blood-curdling bellow of approval from them both. The courtship ritual had stepped up a gear; but the male suitor who hadn't committed the murder was beginning to feel that all-too human emotion – *jealousy.*

Kellwood learned of Bryant's murder the next morning at work. He took the news from Eric Branson, the Night Editor. The murder had been originally outlined by Dave South, the paper's one and only night reporter, who was generally regarded to have the easiest job on the paper due to the singular lack of reportable news in the town during the hours of darkness. He'd happened to be in the Plough Inn when it all kicked off; a couple leaving the pub had run back inside screaming for the landlord to call the police as they'd stumbled over a body lying slumped on the ground with a horribly mutilated head. The newspaper office was in a fever of activity as they strove to bring out a late afternoon special edition incorporating this sensational news. Kellwood retired to his office, too stunned even to accept Branson's offer of coffee. Having slumped into his chair, he felt that he was going to hyperventilate, and struggled hard to bring his breathing under control. He needed a drink, something stronger than coffee; but it was only 6am and he had no desire to succumb to the journalist stereotype. His nervous agitation was causing his left leg to jerk rapidly like a mad jazz drummer rapidly losing control of his hi-hat. Shit, he thought, we were only talking about the dummy murders yesterday, then this happens. Although he had no evidence that his suspects were responsible for Bryant's murder he knew intuitively that such was the case. Branson had told him that the murder had been committed outside the Plough Inn. So the dummies had returned to their old hunting ground, scene of the first murder. Well, if such was the case, tracking them down should be all the easier. He had no idea how this might be achieved and the very thought of confronting those monsters made his left leg jerk all the more rapidly. At the moment, all he required was fresh air; soonest the thought, quickest the deed, and on rising from behind his desk he made his way to the front of the newspaper HQ. He was almost through the door into the street when he was accosted by a heavily perspiring Branson.

"Hey Brian, where you off to? We need help getting this special edition completed. Why not make some enquires at the police station, there may be some additional info to be gleaned, like background details of this Bryant, what sort of person he was, and what cases he was currently working on, et cetera? South has stayed on; he'll go with you."

Kellwood virtually ran through the door to the outside, totally ignoring Branson, concentrating more on trying to stop himself from throwing up. As he gained access to the street and made his hurried way in the direction of his flat – only a short distance from his place of work, so no need to drive – he became aware of the wail of a fire engine; sure enough, not ten seconds later, such a vehicle sped past him heading, it seemed, in the direction of the Plough Inn, just a quarter of a mile away further down the high street. Despite his feelings of nausea his journalist training now kicked in and his curiosity was suitably aroused. He continued walking in the direction of his local.

As he approached the Plough he noticed a thick black plume

of smoke rising from the premise's rear; and despite the early hour, several locals (mainly shopkeepers) were already gathered outside. Kellwood made his way towards the senior fire officer who was engaged in rapidly co-ordinating the operation to extinguish the fire. He knew the officer well, having interviewed him on several occasions during the course of several incidents in the past for his newspaper.

"Jake, what's going on?"

"Bloody hell, didn't think it would be long before you turned up, Brian. You must have a sixth sense. Thankfully, as you can see, we're not dealing with the Towering Inferno here; the landlord went outside to his rubbish bins to dispose of several bags full of detritus from last night's Christmas party and noticed one of them smouldering away. The fire has increased in intensity, it seems, as these things do but it won't take long to extinguish it. In fact – look: the lads seem to have it under control already. Here's Stephens, one of the crew, he should be able to tell us a bit more about it."

Stephens approached with a look of relief on his face. Despite the relative innocuousness of the fire he appeared glad that it was bested. His expression changed to one of puzzlement as he addressed his boss.

"Thank God for that, sir. We were seriously worried back there; thought we were dealing with something far more serious. We still better get the police involved, though." His brow was still heavily furrowed. Jake Gill waited a few seconds until Stephens was more composed, then said:

"Go on, Stephens – what was the problem? Do you suspect arson?"

"Oh, it was arson sure enough, sir. Traces of some sort of liquid accelerant all around and over the skip. But there was something else. When we'd extinguished the fire we took a look inside the skip, and thought we'd found the remains of two humans gave us a right shock. Not much of the bodies left, but there were two heads."

It was Gill's turn to look suitably puzzled. "If they weren't human remains, Stephens, what the fuck were they?"

Stephens hesitated, reluctant to look stupid in front of his boss and the man standing next to him, who he recognized as a reporter on the local paper. After a few seconds he spoke once more:

"Well, sir, bearing in mind they were quite badly charred by the time we'd put the fire out and removed them, and they'd melted somewhat, they looked like the heads of wax dummies. You know, sir, the sort you get in shop windows modelling clothes."

Kellwood nearly fainted; noticing his distress Gill placed a strong hand on his shoulder. "Steady there, soldier! You alright, Brian? You don't look well, mate. Best go and sit down; Bell's Café over the road's open. You look in need of caffeine, my friend." And then, addressing Stephens, he turned to regard the pub once more and said: "You know, in all my years doing this job I still can't believe the crap people throw in skips. Dummies, for fuck's sake." He sighed, heavily. "Call the police, Stephens. If this is arson they need to be here as soon as."

Having taken Gill's advice, Kellwood was seated at a window table in Brown's Café, sipping black coffee, his mind racing with thoughts of what had happened over the last couple of days. What had started as research into a proposed book on local folklore and any possible crime connections was now turning into something real, something current and very horrible. In all his years as a hard-nosed hack he'd learned to become dispassionate when it came to traumatic or emotional events but this situation was starting to get to him. He kept coming back to one question: why had Bryant seemed so obstinate, so reluctant even to entertain the proposition that the dummies were responsible for the unsolved murders of the last three years? He noticed that his left leg was beginning to jerk once more so he decided against more caffeine. Last thing he needed right now was a panic attack. He decided that he'd take the rest of the day off sick, having first reported the fire at the Plough Inn and having checked his emails. Branson would be pissed off with him, as too would be Nigel Galton, the newspaper's Day Editor, who would be stressing to the point of total breakdown over the proposed special edition of the paper. But who cared? He chuckled to himself, thinking how they would cope. Normally all they had to report on were missing pets and fundraising events held by the local WI. He drained the dregs of his coffee and upon leaving the café his senses were assailed by the residual smell of the fire from the premises opposite. He made his way back down the high street to the newspaper office.

Successfully dodging the enquiries of both Branson and Galton as to where the hell he'd been, Kellwood entered his office once more having given a preliminary report on the fire he'd witnessed. He resumed his seat and started up his computer, determining on dealing with a couple of mails before going home. He hadn't as yet told his bosses of his proposed sickie and shuddered at the thought of doing so given the events of the night and early morning, this unprecedented bout of activity. He clicked onto Outlook and the first mail he saw was sent from the home address of one Keith Bryant. It ran as follows:

"Mr Kellwood,

I believe that you are right about the dummies committing the murders but I couldn't admit it in an official capacity for fear of being ridiculed and laughed out of the force. Surely you will understand that. I've suspected all along that such was the case given the evidence that I had managed to accrue, and after my long service on the force one develops gut instincts. I'm up for retirement soon and feel glad, indeed relieved, that someone else will be taking over my duties. To be honest, I've had enough, and wish more than anything else to spend the rest of my days in peace.

Well, that's pretty much all I wanted to say – I'm taking a great risk in writing this but I feel sure that you are capable of separating the private from the professional. I consider myself a good judge of character; I feel I can trust you even though we met just the once. It feels good to get it off my chest. I believe there are forces at work here that we just don't, and indeed can't, understand; as you said, I believe that we are dealing with the supernatural. I hope that your ongoing investigations prove fruitful. Please let me know if I can be of further assistance (purely off the record, of course.)

Hopefully we'll meet again soon, you will be very welcome to our house anytime. Perhaps we could compare notes on this case once I've retired, if you haven't solved it by then. I love the idea of being an advisor in mysteries! Emily would love to meet you I'm sure. I'm a real ale buff

as I know you are (once a copper, always a copper; I asked about you in
the Plough!) I have several interesting brews that I'd love to share with
you!

With best regards,
Derek
(Detective Inspector Bryant, Walden Heath CID)
49, Whitestone Avenue,
Attleborough,
Walden Heath.

The police soon found the culprit for the 'burning dummies' incident: one Lenny Gardiner, terminal loutish idiot from the nearby Brown Hill estate. He had been foolish enough to drop his wallet at the latest venue for his display of hooliganism, and was now being interviewed by Detective Sergeant Hill of Walden Heath CID, who was of an understandably sombre disposition due to the murder of his boss and in no mood to be pissed about.

"Well, it was just a laugh, wasn't it? I'd had a few drinks. I'm sorry, right? Arson ain't my usual thing but I was pretty drunk when I left the Plough. I've had a shit week and felt the need to blow some steam, you know what I mean? I'm sorry about that copper but that weren't down to me, no way. Hands up to the fire, but not that."

It was some moments before Hill responded, preceded as it was by a sharp intake of breath.

"Lenny, I've had a shit week, too. My boss and close personal friend has been killed. But I don't feel the need to go around causing mayhem. Get pissed, certainly; that's not against the law, but shall I tell you what really fucks me off? Having to chase around after little shits like you who just make everyone else's lives even more miserable because they don't know when enough drink is enough.

"For the record, Lenny, just tell me why. Why did you do such a pointless thing? I mean, this is completely fucking stupid, even by your standards."

Lenny sniffed, took his cigarettes from his jeans pocket, thought about lighting up, but was dissuaded from doing so by

93

Hill's expression of disapproval that could have cut through sheer granite. Hill could see that Gardiner was hesitating over his reply but, despite not trusting him an inch, didn't feel that his interviewee was about to spew forth a complete load of lies; his eyes weren't dodging shiftily around the room, he was staring at the table directly in front of him. He also showed no sign of nervousness. Hill was biding his time, trying to make things seem normal, routine.

"Well, if I tell you, promise you won't laugh? I know you won't believe me but I swear it's true."

"Go on, Lenny, try me. You have my rapt attention."

"Well, they were still moving, like. Twitching, as if they were alive but were in their 'death throes' – is that the expression? Big words for me! But they'd been pulled to bits, arms and legs all over the place. Mad, ain't it? Gave me the creeps, too bloody right. How could shop fuckin' dummies be alive? They're just wax. But I swear that's how it was. So I just scooped them up and chucked them in the skip. There was a bottle of turpentine by the fence from when the gaffer of the pub had been painting it, must have used it to clean his brushes. So I tipped all that in the skip and set fire to it. Fuckin' weird, not natural, the whole thing. I just wanted to kill the damn things. *Ha!* How can you kill things what ain't alive? I was pissed, as I've admitted, but not that far gone. I tell you, it was as if the two bloody things had been fighting each other."

Sergeant Hill certainly wasn't laughing. Bryant had intimated to him that he'd believed there were 'dark forces' at work in the town but had never elaborated much further than that. Gardiner's statement seemed to corroborate what he believed his friend and colleague had been hinting at; he knew Bryant had been troubled by the strange circumstances surrounding the so-called 'dummy murders' and that despite expressing professional cynicism – especially to that journalist, Kellwood, whom he was aware that Bryant had recently interviewed regarding them – he'd believed their explanation lay somewhere within the realms of the supernatural. Hill himself was feeling the beginnings of panic; he'd been first at the scene five years ago when the report of damage to old Sherwood's shop had been notified to the police and the dummies that the tailor had lovingly adorned with his

94

various creations had been reported as missing. He'd been only a beat constable then but remembered that night vividly, for that strange incident (made even stranger by the broken shop window glass being on the pavement outside) but more importantly for the fact that it had been when the first murder had been committed. Subsequent investigations and those cross-county that had been linked to the same perpetrator had yielded no clues or evidence whatsoever. He felt very glad and relieved about that, but trails could, after all, be followed backward, and he was starting to feel somewhat panic-stricken. There were things he had to do, but more importantly there was a conversation he needed to have. He looked across the table directly at Gardiner and said:

"Tell you what I'm going to do, Lenny. I'm *not* going to say whether I believe you or not. I'm going to invite you to sit in one of my nice little cells for an hour or so then I'm going to get you to make a formal statement. Then I'm going to charge you with arson, or criminal damage, or quite possibly both."
"There was no need to kill Bryant."

The almost-human figure moved out of the shadows: "My dear Sergeant Hill, what can I say? Wrong place, wrong time. I needed human blood, some life force. Surely you can understand that? After all, we've been through so much together. You've covered for me brilliantly for all these years and I *do* appreciate it so much. You're the only one who really understands me. When I'm fully human I swear we'll be together."

Hill bent forward and lifted his glass of whiskey from the table, taking a long, indulgent swig. It was early evening, and his small terraced house felt so cold and desolate in the gathering winter gloom. "I had to arrest and charge Lenny Gardiner this morning. He found your two 'suitors' still virtually alive but he put a swift end to them. Dumped the parts in a skip and set fire to them. What the fuck happened with those two?"

"Jealousy, my darling, just pure jealousy, they both wanted me for themselves. Literally tore each other to pieces. But they served their purpose... and I have been rather naughty I suppose in leading them both on so wickedly for so long. It was fun. But fun never lasts. Listen to me, I've learnt some quaint human philosophy!"

Hill was now beside himself with anger:

"But what am I going to do about that nosey bloody journalist Kellwood? I've got him sniffing around now trying to arrange appointments to see me. By killing Bryant you've only brought him a step closer to learning the truth. Christ, what a mess!"

"Calm yourself. I'll deal with him. I can always find room to absorb someone else. You're right, he has been getting a bit too close for comfort lately."

At that precise moment there came a rapid knocking on the door. Hill nearly jumped out of his skin, but only managed to drop his glass. The precious liquid seeped over the carpet like blood.

She remained calm; walked over to the bay windows and moved the curtain very slightly to one side. She could just about make out the figure standing on the step outside. Then, turning back to the highly agitated figure of Hill, she said: "In fact my chance has come sooner than I could have hoped for. Fate has brought him straight to your door."

Outside, Kellwood continued to bang the door. He shouted, "Sergeant Hill, are you in there? I need to speak to you about the dummy murders. Bryant and I were only speaking of them yesterday and now he's been murdered by the same method as all the others. It's too much of a coincidence."

Hill was now feeling a little calmer as he moved to the door. On opening it he regarded the man standing in front of him. He said, "Evening Mr Kellwood. Nice of you to drop by. How did you get my home address? Never mind, a journalist has his sources… please come in. I'd be delighted to talk about the murders. In fact, there's someone here who may be able to help us."

Kellwood moved forward into the house.

Outside, it began to snow.

HERETICS, NEOPHYTES AND NEMESIS

They emerged from thick, swirling early-morning mist this fine autumn day. They had been camped in the valley overnight and look well-rested and ready for the task they've come to carry out. At their head is our liege Viscount Zorn, looking grim-faced with an expression that says he wishes he were anywhere else but where he actually is, riding a sturdy white stallion, and flanked by several of his senior officials. Behind him rides the fat, over-zealous figure of Archbishop Xantus Macaris, a man whose very name spreads fear amongst the people of our land. He is followed by a dozen monks dressed in black robes riding small ponies. Behind them come fifty or so heavily-armed foot soldiers, their boots sounding heavy and foreboding as they march along the one road leading into our small town. They weren't expecting any resistance and don't encounter any.

We have lived peaceful lives for many centuries, have never known war. We have always been tolerant of strangers and those of differing religious views, and those of different skin colours – merchants mostly – who have come to our town from lands oversees and made their homes here. Viscount Zorn has been good to us, as was his father before him; we are not taxed heavily and our liege has always given alms to the poor and needy. But a new religion has swept across our land, quickly establishing itself as a mighty and forbidding power. Those who do not follow it or show obeisance are branded 'heretics' and are summarily executed. Fear and terror rage through our valley. Those who try to flee are soon rounded up by roaming bands of the King's militia and put to the sword. Viscount Zorn, along with all the noblemen of our land, has adopted the new religion as the only means of preserving his lands and status. I believe Zorn does so with very many misgivings, however, but the King has decreed that it should be so – he is prepared to execute noblemen as well as peasants. The King is an eager convert to the new religion; and it is a unit of his army, not Zorn's men, who accompany the procession that now draws to a halt in front of the small building where our council gathers. There is silence, broken only by the occasional snort from one of the horses and, every so often, the clamorous screech of crows flying low overhead.

Word has soon spread of the arrival of the entourage. It was inevitable that they would soon get to us, the last town in the valley to be subjected to what has become known as the 'Great Purge'. There are some four hundred of us gathered, virtually the whole population, with Gregory, the elderly, just and wise leader of our council, at the very front. Behind him are the other eleven councillors flanked by the priest of our small church, Father Jiménez, who has refused to embrace and convert to the new religion. His refusal to do so has signed his death warrant and he knows this, but is true to his faith and beliefs. Everyone bears worried and uncertain expressions and the air is charged with an almost palpable tension. Our lord Zorn dismounts, followed barely seconds later by the Archbishop. Zorn seems about to speak but the Archbishop holds up his hand to cut him off, casts his glance quickly around the people gathered just a few feet away from him, and begins his grim oration in a loud, booming voice.

"It is known that you harbour heretics here; those who have not converted to the new religion and stubbornly follow the old, discredited faith, or the primitive, pagan ways still rife in these lands. Witches, adherents to the forces of darkness and evil. Such people amongst you will be rooted out and executed. Those wishing to convert can do so quite simply here and now. The ceremony is brief and my acolytes will hear your confessions and baptize you in the new faith."

There is an outbreak of murmuring amongst several sections of the people gathered; then the sounds of many hurried conversations gains in volume. Gregory turns around to confer with the other councillors. Once more, the Archbishop lifts up his hand and the crowd falls silent.

"Citizens, you have two hours to decide which way your future path lies. Salvation and eternal life in the new faith, or hell and damnation with the old beliefs, whether church or pagan. Now go back to your homes and make your decisions, and may

God guide the choices that you make."

The crowd is about to disperse when Viscount Zorn steps forward, brow deeply furrowed with concern. His voice croaks with emotion and it looks to me as if he is fighting to hold back tears.

"My people, we have lived in this valley in peace and an atmosphere of tolerance and mutual respect and understanding for many generations, since before even my great grandfather's time. No sword or spear has been raised in anger in all that time. Too many lives have been lost in this purge already." At these words, the Archbishop shoots Zorn a warning glance, which our lord notices, but ignores and continues:

"The populations of the other towns in my lands have been decimated over the last few weeks. The smell of death and decay lies like a poisoned fog over the valley. I weep for those people whose deaths I have been unable to prevent. I implore you therefore to convert; save your lives, and we can continue our peaceful lives as before."

The crowd at once erupts into a frenzy of noise, and I notice bitter arguments begin to develop. This ultimatum will drive families, friends and neighbours apart. Gregory and the other councillors walk towards Zorn in an attempt, no doubt, to plea for mercy. But it is pointless, a forlorn hope. Zorn has no authority whilst the Archbishop is here.

Throughout all this, Selena has remained silent and unmoving next to me. As the crowd begins to disperse and the people make their way back to their homes, she turns to me and smiles. There is no need to ask Serena what decision she has made; I can read the look of defiance in her deep brown eyes. This quickly turns to a look of concern as she considers what decision I myself will come to. I do not know yet what I will do, although my greatest impulse is to follow Serena wherever events may lead us. We turn together and head back towards her house, moving slowly as if we are trudging through thick mud.

I am writing this in the hope that it will prove to be a true and accurate record of the terrible events that have blighted our land at this time and particularly this town where I live; I cannot speak with any authority about the atrocities committed elsewhere in the valley as I did not witness them. I have only heard anecdotal evidence. But first I must explain about myself, who I am and what the nature of my friendship with Selena is.

My name is Tabitha. I do not know my other name as I am an orphan; I have no knowledge of who my mother and father were, I know only that they cruelly abandoned me on the streets when I was but three years old. I have been told that my parents were poor strangers from far away who settled here but had to move quickly because they owed many people a lot of money, and their creditors' patience was growing thin. My parents ran away from their debts and abandoned me here. I have been told that they were not good people.

I was found wandering through the filthy gutters of the winter streets and taken in by Selena, who is the town's wise woman and healer like her mother and grandmother before her. She makes preparations from herbs and flowers that can cure human ills and those of animals, too. Many people come to her for cures for aching bones and infertility or to help improve the milk yield of their cows. Her medicines and charms are very successful and Selena is well-liked and respected in the town. She worships pagan gods but also darker gods in secret that she will not tell me about. *You are too young yet, Tabitha,* she will say, *but one day I will teach you all about them, and you will carry that knowledge with you for the rest of your life. They will help you and guide you; we must never forget the Dark Ones. Their retribution can be a terrible thing.* I am fifteen years old now and Serena says I am almost ready. Since I was seven, though, she has taught me how to make the medicines and preparations in the hope that I will carry on her work when she is gone, a time I don't wish to think about. She has no children of her own to pass this knowledge on to. I have told her that I would be glad to.

We walk in silence back to the house, with a heavy pall of dread hanging over us. Serena opens the front door and we pass into the one main room; I will never get tired of the wonderful smell of herbs and wildflowers that permeates the air here. Serena slumps into her favourite chair before the fireplace and I take up mine directly opposite her. We are both silent for some minutes and then Serena speaks. She looks directly at me but her voice sounds far, far away.

"You must convert to the new religion and save yourself, Tabitha," she says. "You are too young to die. And think this: you do not have to be an enthusiastic devotee. Pay the faith lip service only. Keep our pagan gods close to your heart and thoughts. Also the Dark Ones who I will teach you about now that I believe that you are ready. None of our gods will feel betrayed if you do this."

"But what of you?" I reply. "Serena, you have been my mother, teacher and guide. They will murder you horribly, along with all the others who refuse to convert. This new religion is evil, a blight on our land. The King embraces it as he fears he has been too slack and lenient with his noblemen whom he believes have been plotting to overthrow him. It gives him great power and bolsters his position; a whole new state has been created that will govern by terror and bloody repression. It will take many of us to resist and fight it if it is to be overthrown. We cannot do that without your great knowledge." I am close to tears, and my head slumps onto my chest. I rub my temples as though I feel a great pain. Then, the tears come, flowing like a swollen brook in winter. Serena waits until they have subsided and then says:

"I cannot convert, Tabitha, deep in your heart you know this. I am too old and stubborn, too set in my ways to change now. Nobody would believe me if I converted and to do so would invite great suspicion. I would not be believed. I would rather die with my beliefs and be free in death than shackled, even if in name only, to a religion that is an anathema to me."

I nod my head, knowing what her answer would be. But at least I tried. I do not want Serena to leave me. As if reading my thoughts, she says:

"Even in death I won't leave you, Tabitha. I will always be with you, guiding you. The force of resistance cannot be stopped. It will gather momentum like a boulder falling from atop a mountain. The pagan gods and the Dark Ones will ensure this happens.

"Now come, into my private room. I will teach you all you must know about my gods. But we must hurry, time is against us."

We both rise and I follow Serena to the back of the room and through the curtain into her chamber. I feel comforted and reassured by her words and I am already starting to imagine the dreadful revenge that will be meted out to the Archbishop, his clergy, the King and his noblemen and the whole apparatus of the new state. I know it will be bloody and terrible. This brings a smile to my face. The pagan gods and the Dark Ones will unite and be the agents of our nemesis.

An hour later we are disturbed by the sounds of screaming and shouting from the street. I look up from the ancient book that Serena has given me to read while she has been mixing a special potion which she says will protect her from the pain of her execution.

"It has begun, child," she says simply.

I close the book and nod my head. Serena finishes her preparations and I follow her from the chamber to the front of the house where we look out of the window at a scene of utter chaos. The King's soldiers, accompanied by the black-robed monks, have started going from house to house dragging out those unwilling to convert. Those who do wish to do so remain in their homes and two monks enter to perform the conversion ceremony. Although appalled at the rough treatment of the men, women and children at the hands of the soldiers I am encouraged by the number of those who refuse to embrace the new faith. I hope that they will not feel badly about me when my time comes and I admit the priests to the house.

The soldiers drag those that have been termed 'heretics' to a large makeshift wooden construction that has been hastily assembled in the town square. It resembles a low stage and has several vertical wooden poles rising from its planked floor. I can see our priest, Father Jiménez, at the head of one line, closely followed by Gregory and the other council members. The priest prays out loud until one of the soldiers following up behind cracks a heavy leather riding crop over the back of his skull. Jiménez stumbles and falls to his knees, no longer praying now, and he is roughly pulled to his feet by the soldier who has struck him and kicked forward. The councillors are silent, heads bowed, but effect an air of great dignity.

No time is wasted in despatching the growing numbers of the non-converters. They are pulled indiscriminately from the lines and pushed up the steps of the wooden pyre by the soldiers and bound to the wooden poles. Our priest and several of the councillors are amongst the first. Pitch is thrown over them and immediately set alight. I have to look away from this horrible spectacle from our window and wish our house was not situated so close to the scene of execution. The screams of the burning heretics are deafening and it is a sound that I will never forget. I can hear the hungry flames eagerly crackling and cracking the human skin and as I turn to face the scene once more thick palls of acrid black smoke billow into the air, soon masking the pyre. Through all this, the Archbishop sits impassively astride his pony with a huge grin on his bloated face, mumbling something which may perhaps be a prayer. It soon becomes obvious, however, that he has seriously underestimated the number of townspeople to be executed; the raging flames have completely destroyed the pyre – it could only accommodate a dozen folk – and it would take too long to keep rebuilding it or constructing others. The Archbishop calls the captain of the soldiers over to him and they engage in a lengthy discussion. As the screams of the burning subside the captain calls his men in and addresses them; I cannot hear what he says. Then, to my horror, the soldiers disperse and pull daggers from their belts, and, walking down the lines of the non-converters yet to be executed, quickly cut their throats. I turn away again and look up at Serena. Her face is expressionless; she looks as if she is absent in a land far away from this one. I wish I could follow her to where she has gone. Floods of tears begin to sting my eyes once more. I have never witnessed so much death before, on a scale like this.

Three soldiers and two priests walk towards our house. Serena instantly snaps back into the present and goes to the door to meet them. Upon opening the front door, she says in a voice heavily laden with contempt:

"So many brave burly men to handle two women!" She then bursts out laughing. I silently urge her to be quiet, then remember that she is doomed anyway; has bravely and readily accepted her fate. She shows no fear.

The approaching soldiers ignore her. When they are just a few feet away, one of them shouts: "This is the house of the witch. Are you that filthy, blasphemous heretic?" He is addressing Serena, who replies:

"I am she. I am ready to be taken. But the young girl is ready to convert. She is innocent and wishes for a peaceful life embracing your new faith."

"So be it," the soldier says. Turning to his two comrades, he nods towards Serena and they move towards her and start to drag her away. I back away into the house and the two priests enter. I stand on tiptoe to look over their approaching figures and see Serena, alive in this world for her last few minutes. The last time I will see her alive. She looks back over her shoulder as the soldiers handle her roughly in between them and beams me a huge, warm smile, then nods her head knowingly several times, then turns away and is frogmarched towards the town square. One of the priests closes the door behind him whilst the other motions me to kneel before him, and so the ceremony begins. I feel nauseous.

I'm sitting staring out of the front window of the house as dusk begins to settle, a pile of Serena's ancient books on the floor beside me. The priests departed several hours ago and soon after the soldiers returned, ransacking the house and collecting together Serena's jars of remedies and herbs which they took away and burned. I managed to hide the books under a loose floorboard in my room. I had a feeling they would come back and burn the whole house down but fortunately they stopped short of this, perhaps showing a momentary compassion that surprised me. Perhaps they were lenient because of my apparent willingness to convert, although of course they had no inkling of my true feelings. Upon leaving they warned me of the consequences of indulging in any witchcraft or heretical practises but I pleaded ignorance of such matters, saying that I was merely a lodger here. They believed me. They left Serena's room in a horrible mess.

As the sky darkens, heavy clouds gather, threatening rain. The town is deathly quiet now that the executions have ceased. I am saddened to the core to think of how many townspeople have been murdered and wonder how many of my neighbours remain alive. Then I see a girl approaching and recognize my friend Jane. She sees me in the window and I get up to let her in. She has a look of great sadness on her face and I can tell that she has been crying. We embrace on the threshold like long-lost relatives now reunited.

"Sister, I was so worried about you. I thought they would kill you just for being associated with Serena. You are well, eh? They have not harmed you?" she says.

"I am well, Jane. They have not harmed me. Just warned me not to carry on Serena's work. The soldiers who came here and destroyed Serena's things told me that one of the priests who performed my conversion is to stay here as our new priest, replacing Father Jiménez, once our church has been re-consecrated in the new faith. They intend to clear out the church and destroy what they called the 'heretical effigies' and leave the building an empty shell until they install the paraphernalia of their new creed. Those bastards are staying in our town until their evil work is complete, forcing their way into people's homes and treating them as their own.

"I managed to hide Serena's books, and the knowledge they contain is safely stored up here," I reply, tapping my head. "But tell me of yourself and your family, I hope they have all survived?"

"Yes, we are all well. Father feels like a coward for submitting to these tyrants so willingly but he thought the price of converting was worth it to preserve his family. Mother has been in tears since our conversion. They have destroyed her holy book and prayer beads. You know how devout she is. My brother too is well, but he has taken to the forest and was muttering about revenge and rebellion. It has worried us sick and we will not rest until he returns safely."

"He is young and impulsive, Jane. Try not to worry." I do not feel as confident as I try to sound, however, but my friend's eyes have a pleading look for reassurance. After a few moments silence, I continue:

"Jane, you must tell your brother not to do anything rash

against these people. I have a feeling everything is in hand. Our time will come."

Jane looks baffled until I hold up one of Serena's books and then she nods her understanding, smiling broadly. I mouth the single word, *nemesis*.

This night there is a terrible storm. The heavy clouds that had gathered earlier burst into torrents of rain that run in the street like rivers. Thunder and lightning rolls and cracks overhead as if forewarning the end of the earth. I have been reading more of Serena's books but as the candle sputters and dies I decide to retire to bed. Despite the warmth of the house the filthy night I observe through the window makes me shiver. Somebody, somewhere, is very angry. I think it is Serena's restless spirit, as well as the spirits of all those who have died this day. The army of revenge will be mighty and will number very many. This thought makes me feel good inside and for a while I forget my sadness and grief at losing Serena. I will never see her again but I know I will experience the vengeful wrath of her power. I pity our oppressors. Their time will come too. Very soon.

I am awoken next morning by a terrible commotion coming from outside. Have you ever had those moments when you are not sure if you are awake or still asleep, still dreaming? I move to my bedroom window and look down into the street. The scene below is certainly real, in no way a dream. An elderly man whom I recognize as Leclerc the baker is being roughly manhandled by two soldiers. His hands are bound behind his back and he is still wearing his night clothes. One of the soldiers draws his sword and holds it to Leclerc's throat. I hurry downstairs, wrapping my coat around me as I go and hopping as I put on my shoes. Although last night's terrible storm has subsided the streets are still flooded.

I burst through the front door and run towards the soldiers. Several others have joined them, including their captain.

I shout, "Let that man go! Why are you treating him this way? He is elderly and has a weak heart. Unhand him, what harm has he done?" Leclerc looks at me and his face is as white as candlewax and as expressionless as a dead person's.

"Go away, child, and mind your business. This man is guilty of murder. Last night he murdered our Lord Archbishop who was staying in his house. For this he will pay the ultimate penalty."

The soldier with his sword against Leclerc's throat takes this as his cue and quickly draws the blade across the old man's throat. There is horrible gurgling and spluttering and much blood flowing, then Leclerc slumps to the ground. I turn away, sickened and horrified. Leclerc was a good friend and there has been too much killing and bloodshed already.

The soldiers drag Leclerc's body away towards the market square and I run back into the house and am physically sick. After a few minutes, when I have stopped heaving and retching, I sit down. Then I think about what the captain said – that the Archbishop was dead, murdered. This makes me think long and hard, and at last I am able to force a smile. Serena. You are as good as your word and have not failed us. *Nemesis.* I know Leclerc couldn't possibly have been guilty of murder. It has begun. But now there is one more life to avenge.

I spend the rest of the day in a deep study of Serena's books. I feel I now have sufficient knowledge with which to continue her work. In the late afternoon there is a knock at the door and it is my friend Jane. She has a look on her face which I can only describe as pure relief.

"Sean has returned," she says simply.

I invite her in and she crosses the threshold and we both sit.

"I knew your brother would see sense," I say. "I trust he is safe and is not in any trouble?"

"Yes, he is safe, and he is in no trouble," Jane replies. "Our parents are so very relieved. After all that has happened here losing their son would have been unbearable. My mother would not have survived.

"By the way, have you heard what happened to the Archbishop? The gossip is all around the town. Our joy at his demise is only tempered by our deep sorrow at what happened to poor Leclerc. They executed him for the Archbishop's murder. Cut his throat and then burned his body."

"Yes, I saw them murder Leclerc. It happened right outside my door. I tried to intervene but stood no chance against the soldiers, who were determined to spill blood, no matter if it was innocent blood. Someone had to suffer. They murdered him in cold blood. No trial, no chance to deny the accusation," I reply.

After a short silence between us, Jane says, "You are certain that Leclerc is innocent because you know who is guilty. No, not guilty… I mean… responsible." There is a gleam in her eye. "Could it possibly have been Serena?" she continues.

"I think you already know the answer to that!"

Again the gleam in the eye, this time accompanied by a knowing, wry smile. "There is something you may not know, Tabitha, concerning the Archbishop's murder."

"I'm listening. Go on."

"Rumour has it that he was found with his throat cut. But not only that. He had several nails driven into his forehead shaped in the letter 'S'"

My turn to smile. I lift my gaze from Jane and stare into the middle distance.

"Serena has joined the Dark Ones," I say. "I look forward to what she has in store for the King's soldiers. In a way, I pity them!"

We both start laughing until tears form in our eyes. Then we both lean forward and hug.

I retire to bed early with the terrible sounds of another storm that is worse than the one of the previous night assailing my nerves. I jump at every roll of thunder and look around anxiously at every flash of lightning as if expecting to see some manifestation appear somewhere around me. The Dark Ones are angry and I wonder what terrors the night will bring, and what horrors will be revealed in the new morning. No sooner am I in bed and turned onto my side when I am embraced by deep sleep; it feels as comforting as the blanket which covers my body. And then the dream starts; I look on as a witness to dreadful events. But such as is often the way in dreams I do not feel under threat myself. Perhaps because in my deep subconscious I know who is responsible for what is unfolding.

I dream of the soldiers who are billeted in the large stables at the back of Leclerc's house. Leclerc has always been a keen rider since he was a young boy and often still rode even in old age. He kept several horses which the soldiers have commandeered as their own. They have eaten and drunk themselves stupid on the food, beer and wine Leclerc kept in his pantry. They have had a noisy and boisterous evening and are now settling into debauched slumber. Wild animals behave better.

The darkness outside is as black as crows' wings and the rain starts as a few gentle patters on the hard dry ground but quickly becomes torrential. It is accompanied by heavy thunder like the continual blasting of a hundred cannons and forked lightning that seems that it could set fire to the heavens. Several of the company stir in their uneasy sleep and then there is a terrible tearing sound like someone slashing open long curtains from top to bottom with a very sharp knife. The sound is sufficient to awaken many of the soldiers and they stare in horror and disbelief at what they see; surely such sights belong to the most grotesque nightmares. There is a tear in the air itself, like a large vagina, and a plague of demons are pouring through it from the womb of hell itself. The stormy night has given birth to an army of creatures whose blood-curdling screams and smouldering red eyes hold the soldiers who behold them in a fear and dread that no human army could ever induce. Those who still sleep are soon woken by their conscious comrades as the hell-army advances on them. They have no time to draw their weapons before they are pounced upon and torn limb from limb by the creatures. The horrible scene of blood and carnage I behold awakens me screaming and sweating and my heart is beating so fast it feels as if it will break free from my chest.

It is several minutes before I calm down and manage to control my breathing. Outside it is just beginning to get light. I feel cold and wrap my nightgown around me as I rise and walk to the kitchen to prepare an infusion of soothing herbal tea. I am shaking like the remaining leaves on an autumn tree blown by a strong wind.

As I sip my drink the full import of my nightmare becomes slowly apparent. The Dark Ones have been at work again; Serena has made me a witness to their terrible deeds. I cannot feel glad at what I feel sure has been the awful fate of the soldiers in reality as it was played out in my subconscious mind. The horror of it has shaken me to the core. But from the reading of Serena's books and acquiring my knowledge of the Dark Ones and the hidden secrets of their world I am fully aware what they are capable of. I suddenly feel ashamed of my reaction and feelings. Serena has chosen me specially to continue her work and such things should not shock me. I think of my friends and neighbours who have been brutally slaughtered by those bastard soldiers. They deserve everything they get. Such is the work of our nemesis. I wonder if Serena's revenge will spread further to the other towns nestled in our valley and perhaps, even, across all of the land.

I decide to take a walk, and dress warmly against the freezing air. I am no more than a few steps from the house when I see Frederick, the innkeeper, running towards me, waving his arms frantically and shouting.

"Tabitha, go back to your home! Turn back! The soldiers are all horribly slain and the priests have fled! It is not safe for you to be out here! The town is in chaos! The stable boy raised the alarm. He is in terrible shock. We cannot think who could be responsible for this dreadful act. More terrible bloodshed!"

"I know who and what is responsible, Frederick," I say to him calmly as he draws to within a few feet of me, an enigmatic smile spreading across my face. Frederick looks at me in bewilderment, his brow deeply furrowed.

I turn away and walk back towards my house.

KILLING CLOWNS

It was customary in the town of Zemezny for the people to welcome the performers of the travelling circus into their homes every year and give them the benefit of their hospitality. Thus it had been for many centuries, the people only too willing and eager to share their meagre supplies of food and basic homely comforts in displays of superstitious munificence that the poor and homeless of the town could only look upon with a mixture of bewilderment and envy. The people may have feared God but they feared *The Circus* far more; to deny their needs was tantamount to bringing misfortune and death upon themselves and to be thereby eternally cursed. Only the brave or extremely foolhardy would have dared defy this tradition and there were none of such number that balmy spring evening when the circus arrived to beguile and entertain and claim what they believed to be theirs by some obscure ancient rite.

One such worthy citizen (by which it is meant he desired above all else at this time of year to avoid the wrath of the circus and thus live the other eleven months of the year knowing he had done his duty to the utmost in observing the archaic tradition) was Francois Zola, the mayor of the town, who resided in a modest but comfortable house with his wife Amelia and seventeen-year-old daughter Eloise. That year they played willing host to the circus' two clowns, Bendrick and Chalfont, two gentlemen of sinister appearance and indeterminate age who had performed together in various travelling entertainments for many decades. And who both had designs of a rather lascivious nature on the young mistress of the house.

"Daughter, please attend to our guests. They are in the kitchen eating the meal your mother prepared for them a short while ago but may soon require more wine, beer, or spirits of a stronger nature. This is their first day with us and we are obliged to be as welcoming and hospitable as possible, don't forget. Bear in mind the consequences if we fail in this duty. And please offer them my finest cigars."

111

"Yes, father," Eloise replied, and made her way hurriedly to that part of the house where Bendrick and Chalfont were noisily and greedily eating their gluttonous fill. Upon entering the kitchen, she moved nervously towards the table where they sat grunting and slurping and occasionally attempting to make conversation through mouths filled with steak and potatoes.

"Is everything to your satisfaction, gentlemen?" she asked, both hands clasped in front of her and her head bowed.

"Yes, oh yes!" Chalfont replied, grinning. "Everything is most satisfactory."

"Bring us more wine and a bottle of whisky," Bendrick added, "and be quick about it. Tonight our thirst knows no bounds!"

"Yes sir," Eloise replied, and turned towards the pantry. As she turned her back on them, the clowns gave Eloise's slim but firm young figure lecherous, appraising glances, nodding vigorously their approval at what they observed and grunting all the louder.

Eloise soon returned with the required bottles and leaned over the table to replenish the clowns' wine goblets. Both could barely conceal their excitement upon looking at Eloise's cleavage and the ripe fruits concealed within her tight blue dress. Eloise, conscious of their stares, blushed deeply.

"Will there be anything else, gentlemen?" she asked, eager to leave the room as quickly as possible.

"That will be all... for now!" Chalfont replied, dissolving into hideous, cackling laughter. Bendrick too joined in his friend's amusement with a knowing, leery wink.

"Whilst you are here, gentlemen, please feel free to avail yourself of whatever you desire," Eloise said, innocently.

"Oh, we will, young mistress! We will!" Chalfont replied, and nudged his friend, giving him a sly wink.

Eloise hesitated before leaving the kitchen; she was mulling over whether to ask the question that had formed in her mind. Then, gathering all her courage, and despite her increasing urge to withdraw, she asked:

"Gentlemen, may I be so bold as to ask why you always wear your makeup, even when not performing?" Her eyes quickly flicked from one clown to the other, taking in their white faces, blood-red downcast lips and what she assumed were wigs but which looked more like their natural hair: Chalfont's being yellow, Bendrick's a shockingly bright orange.

It was Chalfont who replied: "Why certainly you can ask, my young and pretty filly. It is because you wouldn't like what you saw underneath were you, by some misfortune, to observe it!"

Eloise laughed briefly and nervously, uncomprehending, a nonplussed expression spreading across her face. She then turned quickly and exited the kitchen. The clowns resumed their noisy eating and Eloise could feel their eyes burning into her back as she left.

"Are our guests well catered for?" Zola asked, as Eloise returned to the living room of the house where her father sat reading. Amelia looked up from her sewing, a concerned look on her face.

"Yes, father, all is well with them. They are most satisfied, I believe," Eloise replied.

"Good, good, you have done your duty well, my daughter. Are you going out to meet your young gentleman this evening?"

"If I may have your permission, father?"

"Granted. Now hurry along daughter before he comes to believe that he is no longer in your favour."

Eloise smiled, blushed once more, and went to her bedroom to get ready for her rendezvous.

They sat in the small café in the market square, drinking iced tea. A plate of pastries lay untouched on the table between them. It was early evening on what had been a gloriously hot day. Jacques looked as if his mind was elsewhere, his gaze somewhere in the middle distance, looking as though he was trying to put random thoughts into some semblance of order.

"Is something bothering you, Jacques, my love?" Eloise asked. "Only you've hardly spoken since we arrived here and you look troubled."

His fiancé's words broke his reverie. He instantly snapped back into the here-and-now.

"Sorry, my darling. I am preoccupied with troubling thoughts indeed when I should be giving my full attention to the most beautiful girl in the town."

Eloise reddened and looked demurely down at the table. Before she could ask Jacques what was eating away at him, he continued:

"It's that bloody circus that comes here every year. I hate the way we have to pay obeisance to them, giving in to their every need and desire simply because of some age-old tradition. It sickens me. They should be driven out of here at gunpoint."

"Hush, Jacques, someone may hear you! And you know the penalty were we to defy and disobey them."

Jacques grunted. "I don't care. Something needs to be done. Our town is being overrun by the forces of evil and if no-one else will act to remove them then I will."

Eloise was well aware of Jacques' rebellious, headstrong nature. They had been seeing each other for nearly twelve months. It often worried her; she was not certain just what he was capable of. She picked up on one of the points Jacques had made:

"How do you mean, they are the forces of evil, Jacques? What do you know of them? They are dangerous people to cross, I can feel it. It is also what I have been told of them by my father, whose knowledge goes back many years. To defy them is to bring down great misfortune."

Jacques shook his head, and replied:

"Thus my point is proven! Anyone prepared to do such a thing must be evil! And how do we know what they will do? Has there ever been a precedent set? Has any other town suffered at their hands by daring to deny them?"

Eloise looked once more down at the table, and said meekly:

"I don't know, Jacques. I only know that is the tradition that we must carry on."

Jacques adopted a conciliatory tone.

"I'm sorry, my darling, for taking out my anger on you. But this has really got under my skin."

"I can tell!" Eloise replied, laughing, trying to lighten the proceedings. She then thought of the two hideous clowns residing in her own home and the uncomfortable way they made her feel.

114

Her mood instantly darkened.

"Now you look troubled, Eloise. Tell me... has something happened to you? Has a member of that roving band of freeloading fraudsters hurt you in any way?"

"Oh, no," Eloise replied quickly, eager to dispel any question of wrongdoing on the part of the circus or more specifically any member of it. She failed miserably.

"Tell me, darling. Something has happened to you. If any one of them has hurt or upset you I swear I'll run them through with my dagger."

Eloise was silent for a few moments, torn between telling Jacques about the clowns and perhaps thereby incurring their wrath should they find out and the need for honesty with her fiancé. Finally, she said:

"Well, it's those clowns staying in our house. They haven't touched me, I swear, but they eat me with their lecherous stares. I'm worried about what they may do."

Jacques' face reddened with anger. He stood up abruptly, banging his fists on the table. The café owner, who had been sitting behind his counter reading a newspaper, looked up sharply. The faces of the half-dozen other customers turned towards them. Jacques resumed his seat, trembling with rage.

"Please don't be angry, Jacques, I beg you. I fear for my mother and father."

Jacques struggled to control his temper, succeeding only after a few minutes of silence had passed between them. He looked into Eloise's eyes, and spoke quietly and calmly:

"Darling, you are the most important thing in my life. I would protect you from any danger that presented itself. But I would not endanger the lives of your parents in so doing."

Eloise relaxed, breathing out heavily and smiling.

"Jacques, my hero!" she said, smiling broadly and with an expression of deep love on her face. Then she said:

"The circus will only be here a fortnight. I will endeavour to keep out of the way of those clowns as much as possible, and try to make sure that either my mother or father is with me when I attend to them."

Jacques nodded his head slowly. "If either one of them so

much as touches you…"

"Jacques! They won't harm me, I promise. Now come on, let's enjoy the rest of this beautiful evening." They rose from the table, Eloise smiling, but underneath worried about Jacques and his temper. He acted from the most honourable of intentions but may bring down disaster on them by his impulsive actions. Jacques, for his part, was formulating a plan in his mind, a plan to rid the town of that ghastly travelling horde of demons once and for all.

Amelia was busying herself in the kitchen, tidying up after the clowns had finished their meal. She was an attractive-looking woman, still young at forty, with shoulder-length blonde hair and a slender figure. She dressed well, and wore expensive perfume but the minimum of makeup, not feeling the need to accentuate her natural beauty. She was happy with her life: whilst her husband attended to his grocery business and co-ordinated and oversaw the political activities of the town she spent her days reading and painting. She was a talented artist, and had had several local exhibitions, and had even sold several of her canvases. Her normally relaxed manner was somewhat disturbed however this evening by the presence of these circus performers. There was something evil about them… without speaking or doing anything they exuded a malignant air that she couldn't quite define but which made her feel distinctly uneasy. And those stares she could feel, those evil eyes boring into her as she stood washing dishes, was not her imagination. She felt as if they were predators, waiting to strike. This thought sent a cold shiver through her and she began to feel fearful, her hands shaking as she put clean plates on the draining board. She attempted conversation as a way of calming her nerves.

"Was everything to your satisfaction, gentlemen? I hope that you have nothing but good words to report back to the Ringmaster about us. We have tried to accommodate you to the best of our abilities. We are fortunate in being relatively well-off and can afford good food and drink."

"Most satisfactory, missus," Chalfont replied, keeping up his lascivious appraisal of Amelia's body.

"Aye," Bendrick concurred. "But 'tis a pity that young beauty of a daughter of yours is absent from the house at present. Still, you will make a more than adequate substitute I'm sure."

Chalfont dug his elbow heavily into his friend's ribs, giving him a reproachful look; Bendrick coughed heavily and adopted a bewildered expression when he had recovered. Amelia dropped a plate in the sink but it didn't break. She froze.

"What my friend means, missus, is that you will make a good substitute to serve us. We would like more whisky. It will do when you've finished your chores."

"Yes, yes, that's what I meant, missus. Good thinking, Chalfont."

Chalfont made to deliver another blow; Bendrick recoiled.

"And cigars, missus," Chalfont said, giving his friend a hard stare. "And none but the very best, mind you."

"Certainly," Amelia replied. "I'll be as quick as I can, gentlemen."

An hour later, Francois and Amelia were in the front room, both reading books. Intermittently they heard the noise of uproarious, bawdy laughter coming from the kitchen. Amelia shuddered; Francois, picking up on his wife's uneasy vibe, said:

"Be calm, my dear. They will soon drink themselves so stupid that they will fall asleep, and we can rest easy."

Amelia looked far from convinced.

"I'll be glad when those hideous creatures are gone from this house," she said.

Francoise smiled and nodded his head in understanding, but said nothing. Suddenly, they heard one of the clowns shouting drunkenly:

"Serving wench! More whisky! And be quick or you will know the wrath of The Circus!"

Amelia rose from her seat and walked towards the kitchen, a feeling of dread descending upon her.

Eloise and Jacques had enjoyed a wonderful evening together;

there had been a firework display in the park close to where The Circus had encamped itself and afterwards, as several dozens of people had made their way to the big top for further entertainment, they had gone to their favourite restaurant where they had eaten a splendid meal. Jacques had only drunk a moderate amount which had seemed to calm his temper. As darkness descended they were now on their way back to Amelia's house, where Jacques was hoping that he could receive a further lesson in chess from Francois over a glass or two of port. It would also be a good opportunity to keep an eye on the clowns and deliver a warning if they got out of hand. He wanted to show that he, at least, out of all the people in the town, was not frightened of them and would not bow down to their every wish. Eloise felt slightly uneasy about Jacques and the clowns being in such close proximity but her fiancé had promised not to start any trouble. Her father, who treated Jacques as the son he never had, was also a calming influenced. They walked hand-in-hand towards the house, smiling the joy of youthful love and devotion.

Amelia brought another bottle of whisky from the pantry and bent over to replenish Chalfont's glass. As she did so, Bendrick gave her a hard slap on the bottom and erupted into laughter. Chalfont joined in, and grabbed one of Amelia's breasts. Amelia was shocked; she stood bolt upright, clasping the bottle to her chest. She was shaking uncontrollably and nearly dropped it. She was struggling to breathe.

"Are you going to serve that drink or hug it to death?" Chalfont asked. Amelia, reluctantly, stepped forward again. Bendrick grabbed her dress and as Amelia tried to pull away the material on the shoulder ripped. Chalfont stood up and pulled Amelia to him in an attempted embrace. Bendrick was squeezing Amelia's bottom. Both clowns were laughing loudly as they pulled at Amelia, who had begun to cry and was trying desperately to pull herself free of their grasping hands.

"Do not deny us, bitch," Chalfont shouted. "Remember the ancient tradition. To refuse us is to bring down a terrible curse on this house and all that reside under its roof." He lunged once more

118

at Amelia.

She managed to wriggle away, and attempted to flee the kitchen, but Bendrick was barring her way. She stumbled into his outstretched arms.

"Come here, my beauty," Bendrick said. He was strong but Amelia once more managed to wriggle away. Making for the kitchen door once more, she tripped on the edge of the carpet and fell heavily to the floor, banging her head on the corner of a chest of drawers on her way down. She lay motionless. A thin trickle of blood spread from her temple. She had died almost instantly. The clowns stood still, temporarily shocked by what had happened. Chalfont said:

"Serve the little bitch right for trying to deny us."

Hearing the commotion and sensing that something was very wrong, Francoise dropped his book and rushed towards the kitchen. He flung open the door and was confronted with the sight of his wife lying unmoving on the floor, and both of the clowns standing over her. They turned towards Francois as he entered the room.

"What... what is going on here?" Francoise said, moving forwards. "What have you done to my wife, you bastards?"

"Stand back, Zola," Chalfont said. "Come no further. Your bitch is dead and we hereby curse this house. She denied us our rights and now we will see justice done."

"Damn you and your justice!" Zola yelled, and lunged towards Chalfont and made to grab his throat with both hands. Bendrick deftly whipped a dagger from his belt and plunged it into Zola's neck. Zola collapsed to the floor, screaming in agony and clutching at the wound which was quickly spouting blood. He expired within a few agonizing minutes, gurgling hideously.

"See, Zola, the curse works!" Bendrick shouted at the now silent body slumped on the floor, a mere couple of feet away from his wife. "Now we will wait for the return of your daughter. When we have had our fun with her, she will meet a similar fate."

Jacques and Eloise reached the house. "I'm looking forward to my chess lesson from your father," Jacques said. "One day I will beat

119

him. One day hopefully soon!"

Eloise began to laugh. "My father doesn't take losing very well. Beware of his wrath!" She felt blissfully happy. She took her door key from her bag and let them both in, calling out, "Hi! We're back! Mum? Dad? Jacques is with me. Get the chessboard and the drinks ready!" She was greeted by total silence.

"That's odd," she said, moving into the front room. It was completely empty. Her brow furrowed, she called out again, "Mum, Dad? Where are you?"

Jacques in the meantime walked past his fiancé, moving towards the kitchen, seeming to sense trouble. Eloise caught up with him just as he was about to enter that room.

"Jacques, what is it?" she said. "What's going on here? Where are my parents? They're usually in the front room reading at this time of the evening. They weren't going out; they would have told me."

Jacques put his finger to his lips in a gesture imploring silence. He gingerly opened the kitchen door, then stepped through.

"Surprise!" Chalfont shouted, then he and Bendrick began to laugh uncontrollably.

Jacques could not believe what he saw; both of Eloise's parents lying, seemingly dead, on the kitchen floor. He tried to hold Eloise back but she struggled past him.

"Mum, Dad! What's happened?" she screamed. "What have you done, you bastards?"

"Merely dispensed our archaic but still-relevant justice," Bendrick replied. "And now, my dear, we are ready to give you our full attention. Please, step this way. You sir," he added, addressing Jacques, "had better leave, if you know what's good for you, my good fellow."

Jacques saw red. Without even stopping to think, he rushed to the sink and grabbed a sharp knife. Chalfont tried to block his progress but Jacques easily sidestepped him: he was both younger and fitter by far. Then turning, he threw the knife directly at Chalfont's head; it whizzed through the air and struck Chalfont with great force in his forehead. The clown shrieked and desperately tried to pull the knife out; the resultant wound was pouring blood. Bendrick looked on in disbelief, and began to shuffle backwards, away from Jacques. Chalfont, meanwhile, had collapsed to his knees on the floor, still desperately trying to dislodge the knife. He groaned loudly then slumped completely, knowing that his fate was near.

Jacques' heart was racing. Before he had time to reach for another knife, Bendrick threw an empty glass at him. Jacques ducked, and the glass struck the wall behind him and shattered into fragments. He looked around to where he had last seen Eloise; she had gone from the room, but soon returned, holding her father's pistol which she aimed directly at Bendrick. Her hands were as steady as rocks; she showed no nerves whatsoever, although her eyes were moist with tears.

"This is for my mum and dad, you bastard," she said simply. She pulled the trigger and the bullet slammed home into Bendrick's forehead. He staggered backwards, then collapsed to the floor. She then pumped a couple of shots into Chalfont's inert form, just to make absolutely sure. Then she dropped the pistol, turned to Jacques, and hugged him tightly.

The Ringmaster had halted that night's show halfway through when he had suddenly sensed that something was wrong; something that involved his two principal clowns, who had failed to turn up for that night's performance. After the sullen crowd had filed out of the big top, not daring to complain, he stood in the centre of the ring, eyes closed, breathing deeply.

"Where are you, Bendrick and Chalfont?" he shouted to the empty tent. A mental image of an ordinary suburban house entered into his mind; he recognized the house where he knew that his clowns had been residing these past few days. His eyes snapped open; he knew then beyond any shadow of a doubt that Bendrick and Chalfont had been killed.

"The tradition," he whispered quietly. "The tradition cannot be defied. I will avenge you, my brothers."

He turned and walked swiftly back to his caravan.

Jacques was trying his best to comfort his beloved Eloise; they

121

were seated beside each other on the sofa in the front room. Jacques had earlier left the house to inform the Duty Inspector of the Watch of the situation; he had not wanted to leave his fiancé alone but due legal procedure had to be observed. The inspector had looked agog at the young man, struggling to believe that his friend the mayor and his wife had been murdered. He had instantly sent his sheriff and a constable to Eloise's house to take control of the situation.

"This could be bad for the town, young Jacques," the inspector had intoned, his chest puffed out pompously. "Very bad indeed. The mayor and his wife murdered, along with two performers from The Circus. Mmm... very bad indeed."

Jacques had left the self-important lawman quickly, having done his duty, to return to Eloise. The sheriff and constable were in the kitchen upon his return, assessing the situation and would soon be requiring statements.

It was Jacques who could smell burning first. Just a faint trace of the acrid smell of smoke initially, but then the whole house suddenly burst into an explosion of flames. Jacques, who was seated next to Eloise as they were being interviewed by the sheriff and constable, sprang from the sofa.

"What in God's name... sheriff, constable... get those windows open... Eloise-get out of here quickly," he screamed. But it was in vain. The windows were locked tight and couldn't be forced open. As were all the downstairs doors of the house, the constable discovered. The sheriff tried to smash a front window open with the sole of his boot held in his strong right hand but it had no effect. The four occupants rushed around in panic, but were soon overcome by the flames and smoke.

Outside, observing the conflagration, the Ringmaster grinned. He had applied white face paint, and had painted his lips a bright blood-red in a downcast expression; the perfect tribute to his fallen comrades.

"The tradition," he whispered quietly. "The tradition cannot be defied."

The screams for help of those trapped within the house

reverberated in his ears as he walked quickly away.

SKINNYBONES

Even at this distance they could smell the putrid stench of rotting human flesh wafting toward them from the creature's feeding bowl. Skinnybones was sitting at his campfire eating ravenously the foul casserole that was his staple diet as Adam and Val squatted nervously, incredulously, watching him from fifty yards away. The hideous creature before them was human enough from the waist upwards, but of porcine proportions below. It looked like the torso and head of a man badly fitted to the rear quarters of a pig. A set of large fangs protruded from its cruel mouth, whilst long, razor-sharp claws looked capable of ripping a man to shreds effortlessly. They knew they must remain as still as possible; Skinnybones was reputed to have a poor sense of smell but highly-tuned senses of sight and hearing.

Remaining quiet and motionless was proving increasingly difficult however – brother and sister feeling the need to wretch violently. But their urges had to be fought down; they were here, after all, to find out the truth of what had happened to Rod, Val's partner. Skinnybones' latest victim, of that both were convinced. It could be Rod that the creature was eating now. This thought had occurred to them both but neither felt able to articulate it into actual words; saying it would surely make it true. Besides which, the creature would probably be able to pick up on the slightest whisper.

From their vantage point in the cold, damp woods, Adam and Val's blood curdled. After spending a week tracking this thing down, both wondered what it was they'd found. As Skinnybones closed his eyes and lapsed into sleep, they took advantage of his soporific state and slipped away as quietly as they could, hoping that the howling wind blowing at what seemed like gale force through the woods would be sufficient to cover any noise they might make.

"Simple. We kill it."

This was Val's response to Adam's question: "OK, so what the hell do we do now?"

Adam again: "And how do we do *that* exactly? You've read the same internet research as me. This creature is reported to be hundreds of years old. A legendary, voracious predator. How come no-one's managed to kill it yet? We should have tackled that thing back there when we had the chance."

"Tackled it? With what, harsh language? Or perhaps we should have thrown sticks at it. That creature's smart, I grant you. We just have to be smarter."

Adam shrugged his shoulders resignedly, exhaled a deep breath, not wishing to pursue this crazy conversation any further. Knew, however, that he would have to. They had made their escape and were now seated in Adam's Land Rover, half a mile away from where the creature was encamped.

"That thing killed Rod," Val continued. "Let me remind you – it was me who found his car abandoned just a mile from his cottage, and there was evidence of one almighty struggle." Her voice was rising to fever-pitch, but would stop short of becoming full-blown hysterical, although her eyes were starting to give way to tears. "Human blood was pooled in the driver's seat and spattered against the inside of most of the windscreen. The seats had been slashed by what looked like the claws of a large carnivore. Rod had then been dragged into the woods; the trail of blood eventually petered out, as did the unfeasibly large, pig-like hoof prints of whatever had attacked him."

Adam didn't need the reminder of the nightmare events of six weeks ago, and winced at the recollection, whilst acknowledging his sister's cathartic need to speak of the trauma once again. Becoming increasingly worried, Val had been unable to contact Rod all that evening, despite calling his mobile dozens of times and leaving several texts and messages. It was not unusual for her partner to work late; what *was* strange was not being able to contact him at all. In mounting despair, Val had sped over to Rod's cottage on the edge of Saltham Forest and had thus discovered first-hand the scene of carnage. Having eventually recovered from her initial shock, she had made two more calls on her mobile. First, the police. Second: Adam. Both had arrived within the quarter-hour.

"Whatever we decide to do, sis, we need to do it pretty quickly. We've spent weeks tracking that thing down and can't afford to lose it now. I get the impression this thing doesn't stay in one place long. The research we did bears that out if the legends are true. Just remember, though, that we're dealing with the supernatural here."

It was some time before Val spoke again. In order to regain her calm, she had first needed to expunge the memory of *that* night from her mind. She turned to Adam, looked him directly in the eyes, and said:

"We found it once and can do so again. I've got the basis of a plan."

"Spill."

"We blow it to kingdom come. Ever made Molotov cocktails?"

Having finished his repast, Skinnybones mentally congratulated himself on his culinary expertise. This latest victim had tasted good; the flesh had been young, full of flavour. The blood, a nourishing soup. He knew it would soon be time to move on – seek new humans to kill in order to sustain his ancient body. Skinnybones had no idea how old he was, couldn't even remember being born. He was just conscious of having *existed* for many, many years. Time for a nap first, though – even the physical act of eating seemed to wear him out these days. The thrill was always in the hunting; preparing and eating his food was an anti-climax. "But hey, a creature's got to eat!" he said aloud, then burst into long, loud, manic laughter.

'Skinnybones' was a corruption of the mnemonic *'skin yer bones'* that had been bestowed upon the mythical creature after its first officially reported sighting in East London in 1875. Anecdotally, tales of a flesh-eating, demonic creatures roaming both town and countryside had been told since the late middle ages. As the legend grew, so did the fantastic stories surrounding it, and the terrible powers attributed to it. No human was safe from its flesh-flaying claws. Mothers keen to get their playing children in from the streets at night and thus to bed would threaten them with the warning that "Skinnybones will get you!" if they refused to come home before darkness settled. Few children disobeyed. Piles of human bones and the rotting remains of flesh had been allegedly found on many dozens of occasions. Thus ran the majority of available internet data, such meagre offerings as were available. Sightings would be reported, then nothing for years, until a time when more remains were found; these were, in many instances, put down to the work of an escaped zoo animal, a panther or leopard often being suggested. Skinnybones loved it when humans preferred to blame his killings on roaming carnivores that they seemed more ready to believe in., rather than accept the possibility of supernatural forces being at work. Fools. Still, relative anonymity suited him, but his ego fed on the giddy feelings of power that his reign of terror brought. It wouldn't do to draw too much attention to himself, although – true – he had been rather careless once too often in the recent past. He had often worried that this may one day prove to be his undoing. The capture of his last meal had been particularly messy; Skinnybones had no idea how long his allotted lifespan was but his instincts for self-preservation were still finely tuned. But paradoxically he realized he was getting lazy. Or just too damn old.

On waking from his slumber, Skinnybones resolved to have a tidy-up; burying the uneaten and least-fancied parts of his meal would be a start. But first things first; time for a bit of fun. Skinnybones loved fashioning necklaces from human fingers or toes, looped together by strips of flayed flesh or tendons. These he would often wear for weeks at a time, until the skin rotted and fell away, at which time he would get bored with them and yearn for a fresh kill. Parading around in such macabre jewellery heightened the feelings of power over his victims. On this occasion he fancied a change, however, and quickly making up his mind he walked over to his now smouldering campfire and cast his eyes across the ground surrounding it. In the gathering gloom of dusk his eyes eventually settled on what he was searching for; his last kill's head. Skinnybones knelt down and picked it up; he had earlier scooped the brain out of the skull and eaten that first – his favourite bit. Now, flexing the dagger-like claw on the index finger of his right hand whilst holding the head in his left, he expertly filleted away the face and scalp with the consummate ease of a master fishmonger. He was left with a rubber-like mask which he slowly and carefully slipped over his own head. The exhilaration he felt surged through his body like a high-voltage electrical current, and he commenced a disgusting, waltzing dance around the fire. This felt so good...

Adam and Val spent the next hour in Adam's garage, decanting the petrol they'd syphoned from Val's small Peugeot car into empty wine bottles. Adam had cut an old shirt into small strips which they then proceeded to stuff into the necks of the bottles. By the time the petrol had run out they had eight very deadly missiles. These were placed carefully into an old cardboard box and kept upright and packed tightly with rolls of newspaper. Adam packed the box onto the back seat of his Land Rover while Val checked her handbag once more to check that the three disposable cigarette lighters she'd purchased earlier from a nearby garage were still there. She was relieved to find they were, even though she'd checked at least half a dozen times. But both her brother and she were getting understandably jittery by now. Satisfied that they were now ready, the siblings climbed into the Land Rover and headed back to the area of forest they'd tracked the creature to, noting before setting off the several attempts each had needed to click their seatbelts into place. Both sets of nerves were strung tighter than piano wires.

Still Skinnybones danced his evil reel, any thoughts of clearing up the remains of his earlier meal long forgotten as he spun and twisted in a trancelike state. He had reached a level of ecstasy he couldn't remember having experienced in a long, long time and had nearly plunged into the fire on several occasions, just managing to pull himself back before getting severely burnt. It was the snapping of a tree branch from a little way off behind him that finally interrupted his dance; he stood now, stock still, listening intently for any subsequent sound. He sensed danger, and adopted an attitude of high alert, every atom of his body on standby. He heard only the wind rushing through the trees.

Val punched her brother hard in the ribs, at the same time

giving him a nasty look that could have killed at a hundred yards. Adam had paled to a ghostly whiteness and mouthed the word 'sorry' as a pathetic apology for having noisily crunched the branch underfoot as they'd approached the bush behind which both now crouched, with the still figure of Skinnybones in plain view. Val gave a 'shush' gesture with an index finger placed over pursed lips and rose upright, indicating that Adam should do likewise. She removed one of the bottles gingerly from the box Adam carried underarm and took one of the lighters from her bag. Brother and sister crept slowly to within twenty yards of the creature, Val thinking, somewhat baffled, "What's the matter with that thing, why doesn't it turn and face us?" Val was ready for this confrontation, her adrenalin flowing like a river, coursing through her body with a force she had never before felt; albeit she was still highly nervous, conscious of the fact that here was an indiscriminate predator of human beings. Adam followed closely behind, shaking like a flimsy leaf in a hurricane. Val suddenly stopped, holding bottle and lighter in front of her and shouted at the creature's back in a high-pitched voice that seemed to her to come from anywhere but from within her own throat:

"Turn and face me, you bastard. I want to see that ugly face once more before I fry it."

Skinnybones duly obliged; turned slowly to face the interlopers. What Val and Adam had expected to see was the same devilish countenance from earlier that day. What they were confronted with was a monstrous corruption of Rod's face. The only recognizable parts of the creature's own visage were the red eyes that burned with hatred and contempt; the rest looked like a nightmarish mask of Val's partner fashioned within the very depths of hell. Val choked, spluttered, unable to move. Skinnybones took advantage of her immobility and leapt forward with feline speed, and with one expert claw slashed at her throat. Val gurgled; blood began to spurt from the gaping wound, and she staggered back, tripped over and fell backwards into the creature's campfire, smashing the bottle that she still gripped. Within seconds she was engulfed in flames as the raging inferno quickly sought and found the spilt petrol. Her blood-curdling screams filled the rapidly darkening forest.

Adam too was shocked into immobility, totally unable to go to his sister's aid. His legs felt like two concrete pillars. He merely stood, open-mouthed, dumbfounded. Skinnybones chuckled evilly, and speaking through Rod's grossly distorted mouth, said:

"So nice it is when my food comes directly to me. Saves me the bother of hunting. I see I have one meal cooking already; so very thoughtful. Such an abundance of meat but I really don't think I can manage too much more, I'm still rather full. You, sir, I will have to save for a future meal."

Once more, Skinnybones sprang forward.

SLEEPWALKER

She walks to the back door of the cottage, unlocks it and lets herself out into the chilly night air. She wears only a thin cotton dressing gown but feels no cold; has no sensory perception at all. Her eyes are tightly shut. She has walked from the cosy warmth of her bed along a well-familiar route so that no object has been disturbed: nothing has been upended or broken. She walks barefoot to the middle of the lawn and stops, tilts her head to one side, as if her senses have returned and she has heard a noise from somewhere within the blanket-thick darkness of the night. Then, tilting her head upright again, she emits a sound that starts as a low, guttural growl, but which quickly builds into a high pitched scream that shatters the silence and stillness around her. The scream continues for several seconds and she then lifts her arms above her head, claps her hands three times. There comes a rustle of leaves from the hedgerow to her left, accompanied by a series of short, staccato barking noises. She smiles, and her pallid face animates with life although her eyes remain closed.

The creature emerges from the hedge and scuttles across the lawn towards her on its four long, spindly legs. It stops at her feet and sniffs at her toes, emitting a series of muffled grunts. Then, head upturned, it regards her through small, beady eyes the colour of emeralds, each reflecting a tiny pinprick of moonlight. It has two sharp tusks protruding from its lower mouth still partly stained by the blood from its last kill. Its upper lip curls back to reveal wolf-like fangs. "My baby," she says, and drops down with a sudden movement to ruffle the thick black fur on the creature's back. "My darling, darling boy." The creature runs around her in circles, like a dog eager to start play. She straightens herself and walks forward towards the back of the large expanse of garden, the creature following her excitedly.

"Rebecca Hollis, will you marry me?"

"Sod off, Ray," the girl replied. "And don't call me Rebecca. Only my mother does that!"

Shaking her head and smiling broadly, she had a 'what the hell do you look like?' expression on her face.

"Your loss, *Becky*," Ray said, putting additional emphasis on the last word as he rose up from his mock-ceremonial pose at the side of Becky's desk. "Fancy a coffee, then?"

"That much I will accept, if you're buying, my gallant suitor!"

"Of course, must be my shout this week. I'm sure you paid last Friday."

They both made their way out of the estate agent's office where they worked and walked the short distance to their favourite café, Colman's, in the town's high street. On entering, Ray walked up to the counter and ordered two espressos and croissants with jam while Becky found a quiet table in the corner. This was their Friday ritual, their end-of-the-working-week treat.

"Becky, how do you sleep at night?" Ray said, taking the seat opposite his colleague. Becky looked up suddenly from her mobile on which she'd been composing a text to her sister. "What do you mean?" she replied, suddenly sounding testy, defensive. Ray seemed not to notice the change in her mood. "I mean, lying there at night without the warmth of my body next to yours."

"Oh Ray, you never give up, do you?" Becky said, resuming once more her cheerful mood and enjoying Ray's flirty banter.

"If you must know, I suffer from a… habit? Condition? Not sure what the correct expression is."

"Expression for what, my darling girl?"

"Somnambulism."

"Come again?"

"I sleepwalk. Have done since I was a little girl. I get rather sensitive about it in case people think I'm abnormal, hence my being a bit snappy just now. I hardly ever discuss it, you're one of the few people who know. There's no known cause or cure for it. It doesn't happen every night, though, thank God, but I've woken up in some pretty strange places."

The waitress brought their coffee and croissants at that moment. Laying them on the table, she withdrew and returned to her counter once more.

"Wow, I don't know what to say, Becky. Have you ever hurt yourself?"

132

"No, never. Wake up with not a scratch on me. That's the weird thing. Your eyes are closed throughout it all but you don't trip, fall or break anything. It's as if another sense kicks in while you're doing it. Anyway, let's change the subject. Got any plans for the weekend?"

"Taking you out to lunch tomorrow to a lovely country pub I know not far from here. Just as friends, of course. Pick you up at one?"

"Sure," Becky replied, "as long as you don't propose to me again!"

"Promise. I can't handle the rejection. A guy can only take so much."

They both laughed at this and began biting into their pastries.

Ray arrived at Becky's cottage a few minutes before the appointed hour. He'd been thinking during the drive out there about how good life was for him right now: he had a good, well-paid job and the potential to successfully woo his beautiful colleague. *Steady though,* he'd thought, *don't want to go over the top and drive her away.* Becky had moved into her parents' cottage a few months after their untimely death in a car accident. She still found it painful to talk about, three years after. She had been joined there by her sister, Sarah, shortly after her divorce just over a year ago. Ray parked his car on the gravel driveway and walked the few short steps to the front door. The cottage was typically English, exuding a rustic charm with ivy growing abundantly around the outer walls and the neat front garden a riot of colour from the aster plants whose petals of pastel pinks and blues soaked up the bright, warm autumn sunshine. *I could see me living in a place like this,* he thought. *Maybe here, with Becky...* he shook his head vigorously as if to try to banish the thought. One step at a time... He lifted the door knocker and gave a modest half-dozen taps.

After a couple of minutes, and having got no answer, he knocked a further three times, a little louder. Still no response. Perhaps she was finishing getting ready, he thought. He reached into his jacket pocket and produced his mobile; flicked through the directory until he found Becky's number, and rang. After several seconds he got her voicemail. Puzzled, he walked around the side of the cottage. There he found an open window and shouted through: "Becky, are you there? It's Ray. I hope you haven't forgotten our lunch date. Becky?" Still there was no response. Puzzled, he walked further around to the back. Something compelled him to look out onto the large, neatly-mown lawn; it was there that he saw the sprawled figure of a girl wearing only white satin pyjamas. Alarm ran through his brain like an electrical current. He began to run towards the figure, worried now, shouting, "Becky, is that you? Are you OK?" There was something horribly wrong, he realized as he drew closer. The arms and legs were bent at unnatural angles, as if the bones had been broken. The head was bent to one side and looked as if the neck had been snapped. *Oh my God, oh my God, please don't be Becky,* he thought, although as he reached her he knew that his hopes were forlorn and that he was confronted with the body of the girl he loved. He sank to his knees beside her and gently lifted her head, then jumped up again in a horrified shock that drained the colour from his face and made him retch violently. Becky's throat had been cut, and an ugly, gaping wound crusted with dried blood made her head loll to one side as he released his hold. Not only that; a large chunk of flesh was missing that had once been her right cheek. It looked as if it had been ripped off violently by a wild animal. What looked like teeth marks were visible around parts of both wounds, and there were two large wounds to her chest, almost as if she had been thrust with a spear or sword. A large part of her stomach had been ripped open, and her viscera – or what was left of them – were trailing on the ground. Ray continued to retch until all he brought up was copious amounts of stomach acid. He felt freezing cold despite the day's warmth and was shaking uncontrollably. He ran-staggered towards the back door of the cottage that he now saw stood open. "Sarah!" he shouted, struggling to get the words through a throat and mouth thick with the taste of vomit and acid. "Sarah! Becky has been attacked, she's dead. Oh my God, she's dead." He collapsed in a flood of tears as he reached the door. "Sarah, please, where are you? It's your sister..." he wailed. He lifted his head and stared into the gloomy interior. It was there, in the kitchen, that he saw another human shape sprawled on the floor. Ray's heart was beating so quickly he feared it would burst out of his chest. "Sarah?" he sobbed, no, not you too… no…" Although by now he realized it could only be Becky's sister. He crawled over the step towards her body. She had suffered a similarly fatal wound to the throat, but this wound had been inflicted so violently that it had completely torn her head from her neck. The whole left side of her face looked as if it had been chewed off. She also had two huge stab-like wounds in her chest, as if she had been gored by a bull. Ray turned his head away quickly from the horrific scene before him and he again reached for the mobile in his jacket pocket. Fingers shaking violently, he managed to jab the numbers 999. The ambulance and police arrived within minutes of each other a short while later.

Once again she walks to the middle of the garden; it is nearly midnight, and her bare feet leave a meandering trail in the first light autumn frost that gently caresses the short grass, reflecting moonlight so that it looks like millions of glistening stars. Again she utters the low, guttural groan, again it rises in pitch; again she raises her arms and claps her hands three times. The creature duly appears, breaking from the leafy undergrowth and walks towards her, slowly this time.

"Baby feel good?" she says lovingly, staring into its eyes which glow with green fire. "Baby drink lots of blood and eat lots of delicious flesh?" The creature rolls over onto its back and she rubs its stomach gently. It feels swollen, distended. "You have eaten well, I can tell! Go now, we'll hunt again soon." The creature clambers back on to its feet and walks dutifully back to the cover and safety of the hedgerow.

Ray reached for the whiskey bottle and poured himself a generous measure with shaking hands, managed to get the tumbler to his dry lips and took a long swig that almost made him choke. He glanced up at the kitchen clock: 2.21a.m. How long had he been up? He couldn't remember, couldn't remember going to bed even. He'd stopped taking the tranquillizers prescribed by his doctor a couple of days ago; they were making his dreams – no, his nightmares – far worse. But surely that was better than the waking nightmare he was enduring? His mind was a maelstrom of conflicting images and emotions, and he kept going over the same questions that crashed around his brain like an out-of-control rollercoaster. Who, or what, could have done those horrific things to the girls? What had the police meant exactly at the inquests when they'd read the evidence of the DNA tests on the saliva collected from Becky and Sarah's wounds that had baffled the experts, declaring that it certainly wasn't human and didn't belong to any classification of animal on record? How could that be? It had been over a week since he'd made the gruesome discovery, surely they must know more by now? It was mad, the whole thing was insane, just didn't make sense.

He took another, slower swig of the fiery liquid and felt calmed again by the glowing warmth in his mouth and throat, down his gullet and into his stomach, that groaned constantly through lack of food. He couldn't remember when he'd last eaten. He felt powerless, longing to be able to do something, anything, to help explain what had happened. Knew however that there was nothing he could do to bring the girls back. He began to rock back and forth in his chair, his anguish and frustration increasing until he drained the last of his drink and hurled the empty tumbler at the wall where it shattered and fell to the floor in a multitude of shards. He couldn't drink more anyway; the bottle was empty and he was in no fit state to drive to the 24-hour supermarket to buy more. He resolved to call his elder brother, ask him to stop off for booze on the way. His brother had said to ring him any time, day or night, and he'd be there as soon as he could. Ray needed to talk to someone, to rationalize the thoughts that were crashing through his mind like angry winter waves onto a stony beach. His brother would know what to do.

"You don't need any more booze, Ray. I'll put some coffee on."

His brother, James, had arrived half an hour after Ray had made the call; he looked dishevelled, felt a mess, as anyone who'd been disturbed from a good deep sleep would at that hour. But, as promised, he was always willing to be there for his brother to help him through his present crisis, and had hurriedly dressed and driven across town. He walked towards the sink, picked up the kettle, and filled it from the cold tap. "I understand how you feel, Ray, but drinking yourself stupid won't help."

Ray grunted, sat back in his chair. "How the fuck can you possibly know how I feel, huh?" he shouted, shaking his head. Jack let the comment go and sat down next to him. "Ray, you need to see someone. I don't know, a grief counsellor, a psychiatrist specializing in trauma, perhaps?"

"I'm not mad."

"I know you're not. But these people can help, they're trained. You're not coping, you've had a terrible, shocking, traumatic experience and you're not coping. God knows how anyone would. But you have to find a way through this. You have to carry on."

Ray leaned forwards and sank his head into his hands, saying simply, almost in a whisper: "How the fuck can I cope with this, Jim? It's with me 24-7. It's all I think about. I don't think I'll ever get over it."

"We'll get over it together, Ray. I'll help you as much as I can. I'll be with you every step of the way. I know how deeply you feel… felt for Becky, sounds like given time you two could have really made a go of it. And Sarah, she sounded lovely too." Ray leaned forward again, nodded his head, and looked down at his feet, his hands clasped tightly between his knees.

A silence lasting several minutes passed between them.

"Ray, are the police any further forward in their investigations? That shit at the inquests, about whoever or whatever was responsible for what happened not being human or animal…?"

Ray gave a dismissive grunt. "Are they fuck? All they can come up with is that Sarah must have heard Becky get up and start sleepwalking and followed her downstairs to make sure she was OK. Either that or she sleepwalked, too. As if they would go

137

sleepwalking at the same time. As for the DNA samples, they've been sent to the States for further analysis. They have wider experience in dealing with – quote – 'more exotic species of animal, which may have escaped from a private zoo.' Can you believe it? Pathetic. Nothing of this world killed those girls, James, I'm convinced of that. What other explanation could there be? I know it sounds far-fetched, but..." His voice trailed off and he once more lapsed into silence. James shook his head, seemed to have something to say but was unsure how to phrase it. After several minutes, he said:

"Ray, do you remember Aunt Bella? She died when you were four years old."

"Vaguely. Why?"

"She was a sleepwalker. Often said she could remember vividly the nightmares she had while doing it. I remember her once telling me that one recurring nightmare she had was of a wild, demonic, boar-like creature that fed on human blood and flesh. Scared the shit out of me, I was barely older than you were. Used to keep me awake at night."

Ray shook his head. "I don't remember any of that. What are you telling me, James? That some nightmare-inspired creature has come to life, springing from our long-dead aunt's subconscious and is rampaging around attacking young women?" He shook his head. "Perhaps that's true. As I said, nothing of this Earth killed Becky and Sarah. That would certainly explain the lack of DNA results."

James sighed heavily. "I'm not sure what I'm saying, Ray. It sounds totally insane, I know. But it's odd... both girls had been gored, as if by a bull, right? And their throats had been cut and parts of their flesh had been eaten..."

Ray winced at the words that instantly triggered horrific memories. "So?" he said.

"So what if that creature really exists, Ray? What if it *has* been summoned in some way? What if sleepwalking is hereditary and Bella's nightmare of the creature has been passed on too?"

Ray looked baffled, shook his head. James continued:

"Aunt Bella only had one child. A daughter. She was given up for adoption as Bella couldn't cope. She suffered with post-natal

138

depression; Uncle Stephen left her for another woman, someone he'd been having an affair with for some time and Bella killed herself. You know that much of our family history? Do you remember what that child looked like? What she looks like now?"

Ray shook his head. "No, James, I know the family history but as I said I can hardly remember Aunt Bella, let alone the daughter... our cousin."

"I have quite vivid memories of her. A quiet girl, always kept herself to herself. Very introverted. Her name is Julia. I've only seen her a couple of times in adulthood. Last time I saw her was three weeks ago, here in this town."

"Where...?"

"She's working as a waitress, Ray. At Colman's café."

She repeats her ritual but the creature does not come. Frustrated, she goes through it again. Still nothing.

"Mother, Mother, where is he? Don't hold him back from me. He's ours. He must live. Please release him, please."

The chilly air is still, the full moon is temporarily obscured by a bank of heavy cloud that blocks out whatever light has fallen onto the lawn. The silence is absolute. Then a voice inside her head; shrill, deafening:

"No, Julia. Enough is enough. I have to stop you. You have no right to summon the creature. He was part of my subconscious that is best left buried. You've gone too far. You must understand that."

"Mummy...?"

"Wake, Julia. Wake up."

At these words, Julia's eyes snap open and she stares into the distance, unmoving. The creature, unseen by her, lunges at her throat and feasts ravenously.

THE BOX

Peter Sheldon-Norris was a man very much afraid of his own shadow. His natural inclination towards extreme timidity and nervous agitation meant that his friends and acquaintances were few, bordering on the almost non-existent. His life was lived – if it could be described as living – through prolonged bouts of morbid pessimism and a constant, overwhelming anxiety; in short, his neuroses knew no bounds. Everything about the modern world worried and upset him, from the macrocosm of international politics and current affairs to the microcosm of everyday life on his street of small, neat terraced houses. It was for these reasons that he turned to the Box for help and advice, for a means of making sense of it all.

The Box was Norris' advisor, comforter and god. As he hurried home one late afternoon in early autumn it was the Box he desperately longed to be near, to consult it, to hear its words of wisdom and comfort. He had just been subjected to the cruel and vicious abuse of three local school kids who had found their ideal, easy target as they loitered outside the newsagents from which Norris had emerged. Their taunts and foul language echoed in his ears as he rushed away, shaking his head and trying to calm his breathing. The muscles in his left cheek were twitching madly. He dropped the newspaper that he had bought but didn't hang around to pick it up, so frightened was he that his tormentors were pursuing him and would soon catch him up. He ran the last fifty yards to his front door with a rising feeling of nausea in his stomach. He struggled to fit his key into the lock, his hand was shaking so badly, but he eventually managed to do so and virtually collapsed over his threshold. He slammed the door shut and staggered towards his front room. He needed to consult the Box; the Box would know what to do.

It had a 9" screen which was cracked in several places, and sat atop a unit of cheap, self-assembly drawers made of chipboard and covered with a wood-effect plastic veneer, and took pride of place in one corner of Norris' living room. It had once been an ordinary black and white portable television set, a retirement present to his father who had worked in the same foundry for the same company for fifty years. It had stopped functioning as a normal TV years ago; when exactly he couldn't be certain.

The screen was set into a moulded black plastic frame and the thin, looped metal aerial still protruded from the top, like a halo turned through ninety degrees. To Norris the Box and the drawers on which it rested was a shrine, the Box itself an object of worship. Sometimes it spoke to him in his dreams, sometimes – most often, in fact – during his waking hours, but always when he was at home. Outside its signal became extremely weak and on such occasions when it was trying to communicate with him all he would hear was a low-pitched humming sound and the vague babble of distant, incoherent and incomprehensible voices. He would dash home as quickly as he could, scared that he would miss whatever instructions or advice it was attempting to transmit. It had not tried to communicate with him while he'd popped out to buy his newspaper but he hoped it would speak to him now, upon his return.

Norris didn't bother to take off his coat or kick off his outdoor shoes; he fell to his knees a few inches from the Box, closed his eyes and leaned forward so that his forehead touched the screen. He raised both hands and gently gripped the Box on each side. After a few seconds, he experienced a tingle of static electricity; it felt reassuring and had an instantly calming effect. A few seconds more and he could feel the tingle travel up his arms and from there through the rest of his body. Then a jumble of voices rose, but none of them were clear or distinct. It sounded like the low, subdued conversation one might hear on a bus or a tube train where one recognizes a familiar and well-known language is being spoken but actual words are difficult to make out or understand. This was how the communication from the Box usually commenced. Suddenly a single voice spoke up, loud but calm, its tone measured and unhurried. The other voices quickly faded away, as if in deference to the new speaker.

"You have been a loyal and faithful servant of the Box," the

141

new voice said. "How may we be of assistance to you, Norris?"

Norris, eyes still tightly closed, furrowed his brow and formulated a set of clear images of his experience at the newsagent's shop that afternoon, as if replaying a movie. He began with his emergence from the shop, clear definitions of the faces of his tormentors, and (thanks to an excellent memory) a verbatim account of the verbal abuse he had suffered. This all took a mere few seconds. When he had finished there was a short silence, then the voice spoke once more; this time its tone was menacing, although still calm and measured, and sent an involuntary chill throughout Norris' whole body:

"We will deal with this, Norris. You can be assured that you will suffer no such further humiliation or abuse ever again. Go now."

Norris smiled, opened his eyes, and slowly leaned away from the screen, at the same time releasing his gentle hold. The tingling sensation ceased, and the room was eerily quiet and had become deathly cold. He stood up and walked out of the room, feeling as if he had been charged with a fresh boost of energy. It was as if he had taken a drug that had revitalized his entire system. The downside was that he knew it wouldn't last, that sooner rather than later the old anxieties and uncertainties about life would resurface and he would struggle to cope with everyday life once again. But for now at least, he felt as if nothing on earth could bring him down.

That evening Norris, in calmer mood, sat in his favourite armchair opposite the Box reading a much-loved and well-thumbed copy of M. R. James ghost stories, while outside the wind was blowing a howling gale that sounded like the rolling and crashing of waves on a beach in winter. So engrossed was he that he didn't notice the Box flicker into life: at first it displayed a series of grainy and distorted black and white images with no soundtrack, then the voice that had spoken to him earlier suddenly began a commentary over the repeated images. Startled by the sound of the voice, Norris looked up from his book and stared at the Box in disbelief as the images gradually became clearer, playing out what seemed to be an alternative scenario of what had happened to him outside the newsagents shop that afternoon. The voice was repeating, over and over:

"Police are investigating the cold-bloodied murder of three youths in town earlier today… there were no witnesses but police have been able to identify the assailant from CCTV images… police are investigating…"

The footage showed a man – quite obviously Norris, that fact was clear enough – emerging from the shop, taking a gun from his inside jacket pocket, and firing it virtually point-blank at three youths, who collapsed in writhing heaps and then became still. Norris was horrified; he didn't even own a gun, what the hell was happening? Then the voice recommenced on a different discourse:

"Police have established that the assailant was Peter Sheldon-Norris from the Oldtown district. Upon arriving at his house, it was discovered that he, too, had been brutally murdered…"

Norris broke out into a cold sweat. Why was the Box doing this? There came a sudden, heavy rapping at his front door, and Norris nearly jumped out of his skin. He got up from his chair and walked stiffly to the hallway, still numb with shock and disbelief at what the Box was broadcasting. He opened his front door, and his shock and horror was complete. For there were his three tormentors from earlier on, the ones that the Box was now showing had been brutally gunned down. Each one of them had a gaping, bloody hole in their chest, surrounded by dried, crusted blood. Their skin was a translucent marble-white and their eyes were red-rimmed with pupils as black as midnight. Norris staggered back and tripped over. The tormentors fell upon him within seconds, tearing at his flesh with their bare hands, their nails like the talons of a bird of prey.

In the background, the Box had become blank and silent once more.

THE BURNING TREE

*'There stood a hill not far, whose grisly top
Belched fire and rolling smoke...'*
John Milton: *Paradise Lost*

Cal Hannon saw ghosts. He once claimed to have seen the ghost of Rhianna Morrow, the village witch who had died three years previously, but nobody believed him and threw rotten fruit at him, and Cal ran away crying, even though he was nearly thirty by then, which is quite old. Cal was very sensitive. He perceived the wickedness in the living as well as the dead, or so he reckoned. He reckoned that the living were more evil than the dead who have led bad lives and sometimes come back to haunt us. Cal said there was evil in the village but again nobody believed him except me. That changed the day the Burning Tree was destroyed.

Let me tell you about the Burning Tree. It sits on top of Nairn Hill and is ancient, more so than the very oldest man in the village. You can hardly see it in the distance from the village (the Tree I mean, not the hill) so when it bursts into flame, which has only happened a few times since I've been born, it looks like the hill itself is on fire. We know that when the Tree burns something bad is going to happen, like our crops will fail and we'll have a bad harvest or our animals will die of mystery illnesses; all of which has happened on many occasions as the old generation often tell us. The Tree, when it burns, always means trouble. Arabella the witch can interpret the signs she reads in the flames. But it is also a healing Tree, and the sick and lame have been known to become cured when they lay their hands on its bark, though not when it's ablaze, of course.

We take sacrificial offerings to the Tree to stop bad things happening and to make it calm and peaceful when it's warning us, like a kind of portent or omen. They are words Cal taught me. The Tree is revered like a god. Nobody dare cut the Tree down as it is feared that to do so will make worse things happen because, like I said, we believe it is holy. Cal said that the Tree doesn't consume the offerings we give, they are dragged away and eaten by foxes and wolves. Some accuse Cal of being a heretic. I'm not sure what a heretic is and nobody will tell me, saying I'm too young and my brain is too slow, and even when I'm older I still won't understand. Just because my parents are poor and uneducated. I'm not sure what a brain is either but I know it's in your head and I think it controls the things you do. One old man said once that the Tree will make Cal burst into flames too if he didn't watch what he said and that it was a wonder it hadn't happened before now. Cal always seems to be in some sort of bother. Perhaps his brain is a bit slow too, like mine.

Anyway I was telling you about the day that the Tree was destroyed. It happened the day after Cal saw another of his ghosts. He was out in the woods at the bottom of the hill where the Tree is, collecting mushrooms by moonlight, which he cooks and eats because he doesn't own any animals or have much money, even when Sebastian pays him to clean out his stables, which he's too lazy to do himself. Cal says the mushrooms he likes best always taste better when picked at night time. He was near some birch trees, bending over and poking at the ground with a sharp stick when he heard a terrible wailing noise, like dozens of souls in torment he said, and he was so shocked he dropped the basket he always carries when mushrooming and his heart was beating so fast and with such force he thought it was going to burst out of his chest. He was rooted to the spot, his belly went all wobbly and he thought he would faint. Cal said he had never been so scared before. The noise carried on for some minutes and then there came an intense glow of green light about a hundred yards from where he was standing and there was what looked to be the black shape of a person in the middle of the light, although it had no features, he could only see the arms and legs and head. Cal said that whoever it was they weren't very tall, it looked like the figure of a child. It started groaning at first but then started speaking actual words, and it was a warning. All Cal could make out were the words 'burning' and 'tree' which it repeated over and over maybe a dozen times, but then it mentioned the name of someone in our village who was wicked, the voice said, and they were going to do something bad which would bring disaster to the village. Cal said that some of what it then said was hard to make out and he struggled to understand the ghost-child.

Now the person mentioned who was apparently wicked and would do a bad thing was Sophia, the wife of one of our village elders called Joseph. Joseph is a nice man, and Sophia is a nice lady, so Cal thought he'd misheard or the ghost-child had got it wrong and perhaps meant somebody else. Sophia often gives me sweets and lets me play in her garden, which is nice as we don't have one at home, only a dirty old yard full of chicken cages and discarded junk. Our dog leaves his mess on the slabs and dad gets cross as he's the one who has to keep clearing it up. Sophia and Joseph don't have a dog so you can play safely and not get dirty. So both Cal and I agreed that it couldn't have been Sophia that the ghost-child was referring to. But the warning still scared him, nevertheless. Cal said the ghost-child appeared for perhaps ten minutes and then vanished; the green light just suddenly snapped off like someone had extinguished a candle and the night went back to how it should have been, with hooting owls and the hysterical shrieks of foxes which had gone all quiet while the ghost-child had been there. Cal came and told me this the next morning and asked what he should do, which I knew meant what should *we* do. Cal often comes to me if he has a problem, not that I'm much help most of the time because I'm not very good at sorting things out as I'm only twelve. Nobody else believes Cal, though, or even listens to him most of the time. He gets fed up with people.

So I said the only thing to do was to go and tell Joseph what he'd seen and heard but best not mention that bit about his wife. I said I would go with him. Cal hesitated, I could see he didn't think this was a very good idea by the look on his face. Who could blame him, though? He's had a lifetime of being ignored. I said well at least we will have tried even if we aren't believed. If something bad then happens it's their fault for not taking us seriously. Maybe then they'll start believing you. Cal took some time to think this over but eventually agreed, so we went to see Joseph.

On the way there a thought occurred to me which was quite clever really because, as I've said, I'm a bit slow at thinking through and understanding things. It was this: why had the ghost-

146

child appeared to warn that something bad was going to happen rather than the Tree catching fire, which is the usual way? I resolved to ask Cal on the way back as it puzzled me. Of course I had no idea at that time of what was going to happen.

We walked up Joseph's path and I knocked on his front door, Cal standing at my side. Joseph came to the door quite quickly and when he saw me he said, "Hannah? And Cal! What brings you both here? Come inside. Hannah, you are free to play in the back garden if you so wish. But Cal, aren't you a little old for child's games?" We went into Joseph's house and in the kitchen we could hear Sophia singing softly as she baked bread and cakes. She could see us from where she was and shouted hello. Even though I was sure that Sophia wouldn't do anything wicked I felt a bit nervous.

Joseph invited us to sit down, so we did, and before I could say a word Cal launched into a hurried retelling of his experience from the night before, hardly pausing for breath. Joseph smiled throughout and shook his head, clearly not believing a word he was saying. It was the same look my mum and dad give me when I say something that isn't a lie exactly but may not be true, as I get a bit confused sometimes and make things up. Barely seconds after Cal had finished there came a loud knocking at the door, and the sound of someone shouting for Joseph. Sophia answered the door, wiping flour from her hands with a cloth. When she opened the door Samuel rushed in. Samuel mends things that are broken, like walls and the roofs of people's houses and fences. He also makes pottery things like pots and urns.

"Joseph!" Samuel shouted, "Come quickly! The Tree is burning! I saw flames and smoke from atop Manfred's roof where I've been mending the thatch!"

Despite being really old Joseph leapt up and rushed to the door and out into the street, Samuel following, and Cal and me not far behind. We looked up into the distance and sure enough a thick cloud of smoke was blowing into the air from on top of Nairn Hill, which caught the breeze and blew away further down the valley. Joseph hurried on, shouting for the men we passed in the village to hurry and follow him. About seven men joined us and we walked really quickly towards Nairn.

When we got to the top of the hill, Joseph wheezing due to the effort, we couldn't believe what we saw. The Burning Tree was indeed ablaze, but it had been hacked down. The main trunk lay on the ground engulfed in flames that were so intense we had to keep backing further and further away. The stench of the smoke made us all cough. The stump was just a charred and blackened mess that gave off thin wisps of smoke. Everywhere was silent, no birds sang and none of our party spoke for several minutes. We had no means of trying to put out the fire, and what would the point have been, the Burning Tree was now dead and couldn't be replanted. The magic thing about the Tree was that once it had burned its warnings it always extinguished itself, and you would never be able to tell that it had been on fire. It just carried on living. Now the magic was dead too and the tree just burned and burned.

Then Joseph dropped to his knees and began to wail loudly:

"A great evil has been done! Who is responsible for this sacrilege? They must be found and brought to justice. We are now in great trouble. I fear for our village and our people! O, great Tree, who has done this?" He started to cry. I went up to him and put my hand on his shoulder. He stood up again and then Samuel spoke:

"Whoever did this let them be cursed for all Eternity!"

The others in our party nodded their heads gravely and we began the trek back down the hill.

As we walked towards the village many people rushed from their houses and gathered around Joseph, imploring him to tell them what had happened. Joseph told them through eyes still filled with tears, his whole body shaking with emotion. He used some words which my dad says are called curses and are naughty, so I had to turn and walk away. Cal followed behind me.

I haven't told you about the legend surrounding the Burning Tree, by which I mean how it came to exist. It is steeped in what my dad calls our folklore, and is based on a great tragedy. Many centuries ago, a boy was born in our village who grew to be wise beyond his years. He would help people solve their problems and could heal sick people and animals just by touching them. He could also see into the future and could foretell things yet to happen. He was revered like a god. Even the village witch at that time was in awe of his great powers. One night he was murdered, and whoever was responsible was never caught. Perhaps he looked into the future and knew he would be murdered and accepted his fate, nobody knows. Perhaps he knew that he was not long for this world. He was still just a child, not fully grown up. His name was Matthew. My dad says that murder is when someone kills someone else, which is wrong except for in times of war, which I don't understand. You can see why I sometimes get confused.

Anyway, a huge search got underway when it was discovered he was missing. His body was found in a shallow grave on Nairn Hill, where all of our dead get buried. A villager noticed that the earth in a particular place had been disturbed. So he was left on the hill where he was found although he was given a proper grave and a funeral service. Not long afterwards a silver birch tree started to grow on top of Matthew's grave, and grew into the Burning Tree. Matthew's wisdom and healing live on through the Tree; the rest you know.

I was thinking another clever thought as I walked away from Joseph: was the ghost that Cal saw the night before the young boy who was murdered all those many years ago? Was he warning Cal of what was going to happen to his Tree? That would explain why the Tree itself hadn't caught fire in warning or prophecy; it wasn't the village but the Tree itself that was in danger from something wicked happening. And then another thought struck me. It couldn't indeed have been Sophia that had done the wicked thing because we'd seen her at home with Joseph. I thought that what Cal had heard wasn't *Sophia* but the words *so fear*. Not only was the boy giving a warning about his Tree but also of what would happen to the village when he got his revenge. I was starting to feel giddy and very worried and I felt sick as well but I also thought that perhaps I wasn't as slow-brained as people kept telling me I was, although not my mum and dad.

Cal came home with me and we sat in our backyard drinking orange juice. Thankfully all the dog mess had been cleared up otherwise I would have been very embarrassed, although Cal wouldn't have been bothered. We'd been sitting on my swings for about half an hour, and Cal had said he thought that I was right about what he'd heard, when my mum came out and said that we had a visitor. Just then, Joseph came out onto the yard and took a seat on a rickety old wooden chair which I feared would collapse, although Joseph isn't a fat man, but very frail and skinny. He looked older now, in fact, than he had done earlier that morning. He leaned forward in the chair, hands gripping his knees, and spoke to Cal:

"My dear boy, I owe you a big apology. The story you recounted to me about your experience last night looks to be true. I am sorry for not believing you. I think the child you saw in the vision was the guardian of the Burning Tree, the great Wise Child-Matthew." He then leaned back. Cal looked vacantly at Joseph, unsure what to say, then looked briefly across at me, before saying:

"That's alright, Joseph. I'm glad that somebody believes me now. But what are we going to do? Hannah and me have been discussing it but we can't come up with any ideas about who could have chopped down and destroyed the tree, or why. Neither of us are very good at thinking things… well, Hannah is, sometimes. Better than me."

I thought for a horrible moment that Cal would mention that at first he thought the ghost-child had mentioned the name 'Sophia', but he didn't.

"It is difficult to know how to proceed," Joseph agreed. "But first and foremost I will call a meeting of the Council of Elders tonight and take soundings from the others. And we must consult Arabella, the witch, for advice."

With this, Joseph rose and walked back towards the house. Cal called after him:

"Joseph?"

Joseph stopped and turned.

"I'll never be a heretic again, I promise."

Joseph smiled but there was great sadness in his eyes. He resumed his journey into our house.

Cal stayed until early evening when the sun's golden glow began to fade rapidly and the moon was in ascent. He muttered goodbye and began his journey home. He, too, looked to be burdened with a great sadness. I watched him go and then made my way back inside where my mum was preparing our evening meal and dad was feeding the dog.

On his way through the village, Cal encountered Jacob, the eighteen-year-old adopted son of Samuel, who helped Samuel with his work. Jacob was a tall, muscular youth and a merciless bully who had teased and tormented Cal unremittingly even when he was much younger. Cal was no fighter, preferring either to talk his way out of trouble or running away. Upon seeing Cal, Jacob crossed the street and walked towards my friend.

"Where are you going, weird one?" Jacob asked.

Cal stopped, looked down at the ground and remained silent.

"I asked you a question. Answer me!"

Cal looked up and stared into Jacob's eyes. In that moment, he knew who had been responsible for destroying the Burning Tree. *Cal was very sensitive. He perceived the wickedness in the living...*

Jacob delivered a swift punch to Cal's belly, laughing as the air shot from Cal's body and he crumpled to his knees on the ground. Jacob walked beside Cal and smacked him hard across the side of the head with the back of his hand, then walked away, leaving the crumpled figure of Cal groaning with pain and sobbing wretchedly. But something had disturbed Jacob; he had briefly perceived the light of knowing in Cal's eyes; that look on his face that was part shock and part revelation. Jacob turned back and shouted at Cal, who had still not moved:

"If you tell anyone I swear I'll kill you."

With that he turned on his heal and walked quickly in the direction of home. After some minutes Cal rose unsteadily to his feet and staggered towards Joshua's house, blood pouring from the wound on his head where Jacob's rings had ripped the flesh. Joshua would know what to do and would protect him. Suddenly the sky darkened as heavy clouds obscured the moon and torrential rain began to fall, quickly turning the dusty and dirty streets into swirling eddies of mud. Thunder like cannon fire and forked lightning that lit up the sky briefly in crazy flashes of blue electricity soon followed. Luckily Joshua's house wasn't far. All he could think of as he made his way unsteadily along the streets were the ghost-child's words: *so fear*.

Sophia opened the door and was shocked at the sight she beheld. Cal stumbled into the house and fell to the floor, a sodden, bloodied mess. Sophia cried out, "Cal! What has happened to you? Have you been attacked?" Cal made hardly a sound but merely whimpered softly and nodded his head vigorously. He was struggling to stand up. Sophia put her hands under his arms in an attempt to steady him and support him to his feet. Joshua, who was in his kitchen with the other six Council elders and Arabella seated around the oak table, looked up on hearing the commotion and moved towards its source.

"Cal," he said, upon seeing the crumpled figure, "have you had an accident?"

"No, husband, he has been attacked," Sophia said. Joshua and Sophia supported Cal between them and manoeuvred him into the kitchen. The others looked at Cal in alarm. Sophia rushed to the sink and filled a bowl with warm water and went in search of clean linen and bandages with which to clean and dress Cal's wound.

"I have a soothing balm in my bag," Arabella said upon Sophia's return. "It will also stop infection. Here, when the blood is cleaned away, apply this."

Sophia took the small pot that Arabella proffered and busied herself with Cal's wounds. First of all, they seated him in a large comfortable chair next to the fire. He was freezing cold, trembling. Joshua knew that Cal was often bullied and also knew the primary culprit.

"Is this is Jacob's doing, Cal? Am I right? Don't be afraid. He will be punished for this, I promise you."

Again Cal nodded his head, then looked up at Joshua through eyes bloated with tears.

"There is more," Cal whispered softly. "It was Jacob who destroyed the Burning Tree. I know this to be the truth."

All this Cal told me the next morning when he came to our house, with a bandage around his head and looking quite rough but otherwise alright. Joshua and the other elders as well as Arabella had gone to Samuel's house to confront Jacob not long after Sophia had begun to clean Cal's wounds and run him a hot bath. He had been given clean clothes and a bed for the night. Joshua and the others had soon returned, however, as Samuel had said that Jacob had come home the previous evening but had left again barely half an hour later, in something of a hurry. He had left his father a note, which he had read and handed over to Joshua. Cal had seen it and it had said that he knew and feared that Cal would tell on him, so he was making a full confession. He admitted to hacking down and setting fire to the Burning Tree because he thought we shouldn't be beholden to old superstitions and supernatural nonsense and wanted to show everyone that the Tree was not a religious symbol and shouldn't be treated as such but was just bark, branches and leaves, and we were pathetic weak sheep for considering it to be holy. He didn't regret what he'd done but was running away as he feared the consequences but they'd soon see he was right and he would come back. Joshua and the Council had agreed to set up a search party for Jacob the next morning, which would be underway by now. Cal had volunteered to join them but Sophia said no as he was still too weak and exhausted to go. I said to Cal that we could find where they were searching quickly and easily enough and nobody could stop us. Cal agreed, so we set off.

The morning was calm and bright though chilly after the previous night's violent storm. We left the village walking east, which Cal said was where the search party was headed, so I said I bet they're headed to Nairn Hill in that case, as Jacob may be hiding out in the woods there. After walking for twenty minutes, sure enough we saw people from the village – the elders had been joined by many others, so the news must have spread quickly – walking around the woods at the base of the hill. We approached them and we were greeted by our fellow villagers and asked if we had come to help. Both Cal and I said yes, we had. Then Cal stood very still, closed his eyes and lifted his head towards the sky, looking lost as if he had gone to a far-off place. He was like that for a few minutes then he looked down at me and said, "He's on the hill. He's at the top of Nairn near the Burning Tree." I quickly told some of the others and so a large group of us began to walk speedily up the hill, Cal following behind.

We soon found Jacob where Cal said he would be, but he was dead, his body lying face-down by the stump of the Tree. There were gasps of shock and one of the villagers told me to look away but I didn't as I was not scared; I'd seen a dead body before. It was Joshua who approached Jacob's body, which had been badly burned. Samuel rushed up to Joshua and to Jacob's body, knelt down, and began to cry. Cal and I were near enough to hear all that was being said.

"It looks as if he has been struck by lightning," Joshua said solemnly. It was plain to see the words '*so fear*' that had been burned into the flesh of Jacob's back. His clothes were charred rags.

"Yes, I believe Matthew had his revenge last night," Samuel replied through his tear-streaked face. Then he continued, "Joshua, I've never said this, and perhaps I should have done, but I fancied it couldn't possibly be true but now, in the light of this… I'm not so sure."

Joshua bade Samuel continue.

"As you know, Jacob is my adopted son. His mother, Janet, a friend of mine since childhood, died not long after giving birth. She was very depressed and thought she wouldn't be able to cope and so took her own life. The father disappeared not long after learning that Janet was pregnant. They were not married, you see, well… the father was but not to Janet, if you see what I mean… and the cowardly rat disowned both mother and child. Well, before taking her life, Janet told me that Henry – the father – came from a family who believed that it was one of their ancestors who murdered Matthew, thus giving birth to the legend. It was kept quiet of course and not generally discussed but Henry, for reasons I'll never know, confessed to Janet. Do you see what this means, Joshua? Jacob was born with the seed of evil within him. So Matthew has avenged himself twice, having been killed twice, in effect."

Joshua nodded his head in full understanding, then said:

"If that is the case, then it is well that it ends here and now."

With this Joshua rose and joined the other villagers and Cal

154

and me, leaving Samuel cradling his son's body. We moved back down the hill.

Samuel was allowed to bury Jacob on Nairn Hill despite the terribly evil thing he'd done. Not long after the funeral the first shoot of a new silver birch sapling began to grow on Matthew's grave, so in a few years' time we'll have a new Burning Tree to warn us and heal us and I'll be grown up and probably a bit more clever by then. Cal worried that Jacob would come back and haunt him and seek his vengeance for telling Joshua what he'd done, despite his having made the confession in his letter. Once a bully always a bully, Cal said.

As I mentioned at the beginning, Cal believed the living were more evil than the dead who lead bad lives and sometimes come back to haunt us. But Cal feared them nonetheless.

Also from Parallel Universe Publications

HAUNTED GRAVE by Ezeiyoke Chukwunonso
ISBN: 978-0-9935742-3-8

INTO THE DARK by Andrew Jennings
ISBN: 978-0-9935742-5-2

TOUGH GUYS by Adrian Cole
ISBN: 978-0-9935742-2-1

CLASSIC WEIRD 2 selected by David A. Riley
ISBN: 978-0-9932888-4-5

OTHER VISIONS OF HEAVEN AND HELL by Jessica Palmer
ISBN: 978-0-9935742-1-4

A SAUCERFUL OF SECRETS by Andrew Darlington
ISBN: 978-0-9935742-0-7

THE WINTER HUNT AND OTHER STORIES
by Steve Lockley & Paul Lewis
ISBN: 978-0-9932888-9-0

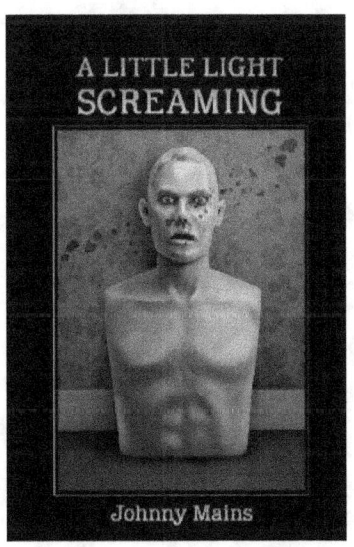

A LITTLE LIGHT SCREAMING by Johnny Mains
ISBN: 978-0-9932888-5-2

ENGLAND 'B': 90 MINUTES OF HELL by Richard Staines
ISBN: 978-0-9932888-7-6

AND NOBODY LIVED HAPPILY EVER AFTER by Kate Farrell
ISBN: 978-0-9932888-8-3

FISHHEAD; THE DARKER TALES OF IRVIN S. COBB
ISBN: 978-0-9935742-4-5

KITCHEN SINK GOTHIC: Selected by David and Linden Riley
ISBN: 978-0-9932888-3-8

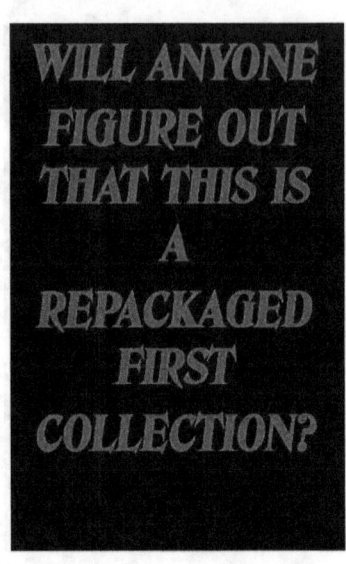

WILL ANYONE FIGURE OUT THAT THIS IS A REPACKAGED FIRST
COLLECTION? by Johnny Mains
ISBN: 978-0-9574535-7-9

BLACK CEREMONIES by Charles Black
ISBN: 978-0-9574535-5-5

HIS OWN MAD DEMONS:
DARK TALES FROM DAVID A. RILEY
ISBN: 978-0-9574535-8-6

THEIR CRAMPED DARK WORLD by David A. Riley
ISBN: 978-0-9574535-9-3

THE HEAVEN MAKER AND OTHER GRUESOME TALES
by Craig Herbertson
ISBN: 978-0-9932888-2-1

GOBLIN MIRE by David A. Riley
ISBN: 978-0-9574535-4-8

THINGS THAT GO BUMP IN THE NIGHT
selected by Douglas Draa and David A. Riley
ISBN: 978-0-9574535-6-2

CLASSIC WEIRD selected David A. Riley
ISBN: 978-0-9574535-3-1

MOLOCH'S CHILDREN by David A. Riley
ISBN: 978-0-9932888-1-4

Check our website:

http://paralleluniversepublications.blogspot.co.uk/

www.ingramcontent.com/pod-product-compliance
Lightning Source LLC
Chambersburg PA
CBHW070038260626
47159CB00005B/2069